THE VAMPIRE MAN

Conway Jackson, amateur criminologist, receives a disturbing letter from his uncle, Sir James Gleeson, informing him that he feels himself to be in terrible danger, and imploring him to come to his country manor. Unfortunately, the letter has taken some time to reach him, and it shows unmistakable signs of having been steamed open. On his arrival, Jackson learns that his uncle was found strangled in his bedroom the night before — by what appears to be an inhuman monster that is destined not to stop at a single victim . . .

GERALD VERNER

THE
VAMPIRE
MAN

Complete and Unabridged

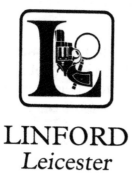

LINFORD
Leicester

First published in Great Britain

First Linford Edition
published 2018

A catalogue record for this book is available
from the British Library.

ISBN 978–1–4448–3764–3

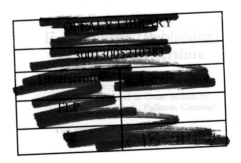

1

Terror Comes by Night

Gleeson Manor lay bathed in all the splendour of a June night. Typically Georgian in its conception, it presented a picture of solidity combined with a certain dignified serenity. A circular drive lined with tall poplar trees, beyond which could be dimly distinguished neat flower-beds — each a riot of blossom — formed the approach to this stately home; and onto it looked the windows of the massive three-storeyed building which stood out raggedly against a brilliant sky.

Not a leaf stirred; and such was the stillness that the church clock in Hamlin Hollow — the tiny village situated in the valley some three miles away, at the foot of the steep incline upon which the manor was built — sounded clearly audible as its soft silvery note proclaimed the hour of midnight.

At the back, the view was even more attractive than at the front. The well-kept lawns, which in a few weeks' time would in all likelihood be burnt and parched, were now at their best. The trees also — a belt of which ran horizontally across the foot of the kitchen garden — were decked out in all the glorious foliage which belongs only to those first few weeks of summer. A thing of restful beauty was this night; yet to one man it carried death in every shadow!

Sir James Gleeson, Baronet, the owner of this magnificent mansion and the last of the line of Gleesons who had occupied it since the early eighteenth century, paced his study, his fingers nervously clenching and unclenching themselves and his face drawn and haggard with anxiety. The heavy oak-studded door was locked on the inside, and the rather sombre apartment lit only by a shaded lamp, which stood upon the massive writing desk.

Although agitation can never be a very attractive thing, it was quite easy to see that this present owner of Gleeson

Manor, despite his sixty years of age, was still a very handsome man. His thick white hair, together with his lean, almost boyish figure and long, sensitive face, showed him to be the unusual combination of an artist and an athlete. Had it not been for his chin, he would have been exceptionally good-looking. This, unfortunately, was weak. But then apparently that had always been the curse of the Gleesons, Sir James being no exception.

With imploring eyes, he glanced towards the ornate clock upon the mantelpiece, as though in some curious way he hoped by the sheer urgency of his desire to make the hands move more quickly. How interminable were those minutes, when every creak sent his heart pounding away at twice its normal rate!

He daren't go to bed because he was afraid. He could admit it now. In his study, behind that heavy bolted door, was the one place where he felt safe. If only Jaggers would come! That wire he'd received from his nephew apologising and explaining at the same time that he 'couldn't make it' until the following evening had come like a blow in the face; whilst this subsequent discovery that the envelope had quite patently been steamed open before reaching him served to increase his feelings of trepidation.

Helping himself to a stiff whisky, which he took from a cabinet in one of the dark corners of the room, he lit a cigar with trembling fingers and fell to pacing up and down the carpet afresh. It was while he was facing the door that it happened!

Behind the desk, the heavy curtains that concealed the French windows moved, almost imperceptibly. Had there been the slightest breeze, which there was not, it might have warned him that the windows he'd so carefully locked had been cunningly opened. Through the centre of the curtains slithered a hand. Soft though it was, and rounded like a woman's in its white glove, the sight of it was sufficient to strike an ice-cold chill to the heart of the man who at that moment turned and saw it. A second later the room was plunged into darkness.

Noiselessly the curtains parted and, outlined against the opaque gloom outside, there appeared the silhouette of the 'thing' he'd been dreading: a horrible obscene shape that advanced towards him, with a swift and soundless tread across the carpet.

Frenziedly, Sir James struggled with the doorknob. But his fingers seemed to have suddenly gone limp, whilst his dry throat refused to give utterance to the blind terror that threatened to choke him. Without warning, the figure sprang upon him! 'Sprang' is the only word to describe the agility with which this terrible creature, half-human, half-animal, propelled itself through the air. As the now gloveless fingers sought his throat, he managed to utter one blood-curdling scream. But it was the last sound he ever made!

The soft fingers, which at first seemed about to caress him, all at once transformed themselves into steel tentacles. A wild struggle for breath ensued, coupled with a feeling as though his head were about to burst. This was followed by sudden blackness stabbed with flashes of orange flame. And then — nothing!

Without uttering a sound, the 'thing' let the remains of what had only a few seconds before been a living, breathing man sink to the floor; and made its way, with the same uncanny noiseless tread, back towards the window whence it had come. Already voices sounded near at hand, and footsteps could be heard pattering in the direction of the study.

Carefully closing the curtains, the vampire shape shuffled out into the darkness and became one with it.

By this time, the house was alive with excited cries and questioning voices, and to these was soon added the sound of fists hammering upon the door. Outside, the night remained tranquil as before; except that in the distance, barely heard above all the uproar, came the melancholy howling of a dog . . .

2

Conway Jackson

The little village of Hamlin Hollow nestled drowsily in its valley. It consisted of a picturesque group of cottages interspersed with one or two red-brick buildings and a single stone edifice which, so the lamp hanging in its porch proclaimed, was the local police station.

As Conway Jackson's immaculate Alvis sports car slid gently down the slope into the main street, he awoke from the deep reverie into which he had fallen, and looked out. His first glimpse of this quaint little spot, set against the white of the chalk downs, which were in their turn surmounted by the blazing blue of a cloudless sky, struck him as being wholly enchanting. Town dweller though he was, by nature the tiny cluster of buildings, devoid even of the familiar super-cinema, held an irresistible appeal of which he was

7

immediately sensible.

Passing the police station on his right, he glanced at his wristwatch, and his face at once took on a seraphic smile. Those little hands, placed as they were at that precise moment, carried only one message — 'they're open'! And as though in answer to his desire, he found himself at the very next bend in sight of the Kentish Arms. A minute later he had drawn up. Climbing out, he made his way without more ado through the door marked 'saloon' into the cool, dark room beyond.

The Kentish Arms happened to be the only hostel the village boasted — that was, if you overlooked one or two four-ale bars that were scarcely worth mentioning; but for all that, it could scarcely be described as spacious. In fact, if the truth were told, at the busiest time of the day it was almost impossible to get anywhere within the region of the bar at all.

On the evening of Conway Jackson's initial visit there, however, the saloon was practically empty, while the feeble murmur penetrating through the thin wooden partition that divided it from the public bar gave the impression that there the state of affairs was much the same.

'You see, sir, now's the slack time,' the barmaid explained in answer to his comment upon this fact, raising her eyebrows questioningly as she waited for his order.

'Pale ale, please,' he said, lighting a cigarette and resting his elbow upon the mahogany counter.

Leaning forward so as to get a better view of her sleek dark hair and trim figure, Jackson fell to wondering idly why there should ever be a 'slack time' when so charming a piece of femininity was ready to administer to one's needs.

He was still debating upon this point when the woman placed his glass of golden liquid before him. And as her eyes met his, she coloured prettily, guessing with true womanly intuition the tenor of his thoughts. Handing her a two-shilling piece, he waited for her to bring him his change, and then tried to draw her into conversation. This proved even simpler than he'd anticipated. And soon they were well away, the woman listening with rapt attention to a graphic account of his journey from Scotland, where he told her he had been spending a holiday with some friends.

As the conversation progressed, giving her a chance to interpolate one or two remarks, he was surprised to find her far more intelligent than her slightly doll-like prettiness had led him to suspect. Little did he realise, for all that, as he stood chatting with her on that sunny June evening, how useful she was going to prove to him in the near future.

As far as the woman herself was concerned, she could do nothing but marvel at the piece of good fortune that had sent such a good-looking and obviously well-bred young man to their village. And in his perfectly tailored flannels, with his pleasantly indolent voice and general air of nonchalance, he cut a very dashing figure indeed! His twenty-eight years sat lightly upon him, and his easy charm proved quite irresistible to the barmaid, who had known little beyond the kind-hearted but more or less rough and ready people of Hamlin Hollow.

'Now it's about time you did a bit of talking for a change,' he suggested at last with a laugh. 'Tell me about yourself.'

The woman smiled shyly. 'There's nothing much to tell,' she replied modestly.

'I'm sure there is. Come now, don't be shy.' His smile was very winning. 'What's your name?'

'Judy — '

He stopped her with a quick gesture.

'Oh, no, don't tell me the surname. Judy's quite good enough for me. And a very pretty name too.'

'D'you think so?' she enquired, rather flattered by this artless compliment.

'Here's to you, Judy.' He raised his glass and disposed of the few remaining dregs at a gulp. 'My name is Jackson — Conway Jackson. But all my friends call me Jaggers. I hope you will, too, will you?'

Judy nodded, the wave of crimson having once again suffused her cheeks.

'Good.'

'Will you be staying long in these parts, d'you think?' she asked him timidly.

'I don't expect so. I never stay long

anywhere. I've come over to see my uncle. Haven't set eyes on the old boy for years. He suddenly sent for me — can't think what for. Here, perhaps you know him? His place is only a few miles out of the village. Gleeson is the name. Sir James Gleeson. He lives — ' He stopped abruptly and looked at Judy in surprise. 'Why, whatever's the matter?'

Her cheeks had upon the instant grown strangely pale, while her naturally large eyes seemed to have opened even wider in horrified astonishment.

'Have I said anything to upset you?' he persisted when she failed to answer him.

'No — no, of course not,' she murmured in confusion.

'Then why — ?'

'Please don't ask me,' she pleaded. 'I — I — '

She was saved from further embarrassment at that moment by the entrance of a massive figure of a man who, as Jackson surmised correctly, turned out to be the proprietor.

'D'you mind goin' into t'other bar for a bit, Jude?' he asked in a voice as mighty as his physique while Jackson shuddered mentally at the ugly abbreviation. 'There's a friend o' yours in there as bin askin' for you for the past 'alf hour.'

'Certainly, Father.' With a faint smile at Jackson, she slipped through the curtained recess into the room behind.

The big man came forward with a friendly grin. 'Anythin' I can get for you, sir?' he enquired genially.

But Jackson's appetite for beer had departed, and with a brief 'good night' he made his way out into the sunset again.

As he pressed his foot down on the self-starter, and the expensive streamlined car quivered with sudden life, he was filled with a vague sense of foreboding. Why had Judy behaved so oddly when he'd mentioned his uncle just now? And what could be the connection between that and the note he'd received?

Had he not been so lost in thought concerning these details, he might have observed the hoarding outside the little newspaper shop. But he did not. And so it came about that the news of his uncle's death was broken to him in quite a different manner.

As he breasted the steep slope that led to Gleeson Manor, his brow became furrowed with perplexity. At any other time, a mild flirtation such as he had just indulged in at the Kentish Arms would have amused him greatly. Those sorts of things always did; it was only when they showed signs of getting serious that he thought of retreat. On this occasion, however, the whole incident was wiped clean from his mind, for his thoughts persisted in reverting to that urgent message that had been responsible for his hurried leave-taking of his friends in Scotland.

'Dear Jaggers,' it had read, 'I expect you will be very surprised to hear from me after all these years, but I am faced with a terrible danger. I can't explain it in writing; it's too nebulous and fantastic. But for all that, I assure you it is very real to me! Please come to the manor at once. I have heard of your interests in criminology, and unless I'm greatly mistaken, you will find ample opportunity for exercising them here. I implore you not to fail me; only be sure you do not bring anybody with you, not even a valet. This is a matter of gravest importance.' His uncle's rambling signature had completed it.

It took some time to reach him where he was staying in Scotland. But when at last it did find him, he was immediately struck by the fact that the envelope showed unmistakable signs of having been steamed open. At first he was inclined to attribute this to his valet, who, as he had been taught by past experiences, was not in any way above such things; but now he began to wonder if perhaps there was some more sinister explanation.

His uncle — and his memory was quite clear upon this point — had always been highly strung and imaginative; more so, in fact, than any of the other relations on his mother's side of the family. Sir James, so they declared, was a dilettante, a dreamer, and a man with artistic leanings who lacked any creative ability of his own; although even they were bound to admit that he could and did appreciate the work of others. Despite his unpopularity with the rest of them, he and Jackson had been the best of friends during the latter's youth; and it was only on account of the cordial dislike entertained for him by Jackson's father that the friendship was ever discontinued.

Now Jackson's father, as the vast fortune he left to his son testified, was a man with a strictly commercialised mentality. To him the city was his whole life. And so it was only consistent with the rest of his character that he should have a rooted objection to his son and heir taking an interest in all 'this art rubbish', as he termed it. In accordance with these principles, no sooner had the time arrived for Jackson to leave college than he found himself forced willy-nilly to enter the business, only to sell it as a 'going concern' a few months later after his father's death.

This sale left the boy, then only twenty-two, a free agent, with the result that he soon became the objective of numerous adventuresses. With his good looks and fabulous wealth, he was of course an obvious target. But not one of them gained what she was after, for to Conway Jackson freedom in all things was the very essence of living. He hated work, and was not frightened to admit as much. Only one thing could rouse him to any outward show of animation, and that was the study of criminology. As an amateur criminologist, he was brilliant and inexhaustible: the terror of every criminal who had ever come into contact with him, and upon more than one occasion an invaluable asset to the forces of justice. It was not surprising, therefore, that the present happenings had already begun to pique his curiosity and arouse in him all the latent instinct of the hunter.

An abrupt bend in the road ahead forced him to apply his brakes hastily, and on rounding it he found laid out before him the magnificent prospect of Gleeson Manor. From the village one approached it at the back; and the first thing he noted was a minute vine-covered cottage which, as he afterwards learned, was inhabited by the gardener.

The next object his gaze fell upon was a

thick belt of beech trees, through the dull red foliage of which he glimpsed the manor itself. This being his first visit, Sir James having spent most of his time at his town house during their former association, he was particularly struck by the gentle peacefulness of it all; and he slowed down the sports car in order to appreciate the glowing spectacle to the full.

Deeply satisfied by what he saw, his gaze instinctively turned once more to the cottage, just in time to see a figure emerging from it. Even at this distance, the bowler hat, at strange variance with its rural surroundings, proclaimed the sex of the wearer; but when the man removed it and turned, as though idly scanning the road, Jackson let out a cry of surprise.

'Hi!' he shouted loudly as he drew to a standstill by a wicket gate giving onto the road.

The man looked in the direction whence had issued this peremptory greeting, and his face at once broke into a broad grin as with unlooked-for agility in one of his ample proportions he sprinted towards the new arrival. 'Bless my soul, if it isn't Jaggers!' he exclaimed heartily, if a little breathlessly, as he threw open the gate and jumped on to the running-board. 'What on earth are you doing in this part of the world?'

Jackson grinned also. These two men, so sharply divided by age and temperament, nevertheless possessed the most flawless understanding of each other, and he was every bit as delighted to see Inspector Charteris as the Yard man was to see him.

'I might ask the same question of you,' he countered.

'Well, in my case that's easily answered,' retorted the inspector readily. 'I'm here on business.'

Jackson's face clouded on the instant. 'Business?' he echoed.

'Yes. Now tell me what you're doing.'

'I'm here on business too. I've come to see my uncle.'

It was the inspector's turn to become serious this time. 'You don't mean — ?' he began.

'Sir James Gleeson. Why do you look so

alarmed? Has anything happened to him?'

'I'm afraid it has,' the inspector answered grimly. 'I'm sorry, but you're in for a bit of a shock, Jaggers. You see, your uncle was murdered last night!'

'Murdered?'

'Strangled!'

Checking the exclamation that rose to his lips, Jackson gripped hold of the steering wheel until his knuckles gleamed white through the taut flesh. Mechanically he nodded to signify that he'd heard; for indeed there seemed nothing left to say. So his premonition of disaster had been justified! And he had come too late!

In silence he looked again towards the manor, now like some fairy palace in the golden sunlight. Was it possible that tragedy could lurk in so beautiful an abode? he asked himself incredulously.

That it was, had been demonstrated only a few hours previously; and although he did not suspect it then, that 'beautiful abode' harboured at the very moment an inhuman monster that was destined not to stop at a single victim!

3

The Telegram

Bringing himself back to the world of mundane things, Jackson turned to his companion. 'Hop in and tell me all about it,' he invited, 'while I drive round to the front.'

The burly inspector complied with alacrity, seating himself beside the driver. 'I say, Jaggers,' he exclaimed in his blunt good-natured way a few seconds after they'd started, 'I hope this hasn't upset you? Were you very friendly with Sir James?'

'Haven't seen him for over eight years,' Jackson replied laconically. 'It only happened last night, you said? How is it you're here so soon?'

'The chief constable at Hamlin Hollow decided that it was a bit too tricky for them to tackle alone,' Charteris explained, not without a slight trace of self-aggrandisement, 'so he called in the Yard right away.'

'I suppose Uncle James was a bit of a celebrity round these parts,' the other went on ruminatively. 'Have the papers got hold of this, by the way?'

Charteris nodded. 'Had a whole batch of them down this morning. I'm surprised you didn't see the announcement on the hoardings.'

'I never looked; and I haven't seen a paper all day. I expect that's where Judy found out about it, though!'

'Judy? Who's Judy?'

Concisely Jackson told him of the scene at the Kentish Arms. By this time they had turned in at the heavy wrought-iron gates, and were making their leisurely progress up the broad drive to the house itself.

Stopping before the ornate portico, the inspector was the first to alight. And mounting the flight of stone steps, he pulled at an aged fixture beside the door, which sent a restless clanging echoing and re-echoing throughout the entire building.

When Jackson reached his side, the butler, an unpleasant rat-faced little man, had appeared, and he made himself known only to be told at once that he was expected.

'I will tell her ladyship that you have arrived, sir,' the butler informed him in deferential tones, 'although I'm sorry to say it may be some little while before she is able to receive you.'

'Of course. I quite understand,' Jackson assured him sympathetically. 'I hope you'll tell her ladyship not to worry herself on my account; and convey my very sincere condolences to her, will you?'

'Thank you; I will, sir.' With a deep bow, the man retired, making his way up the broad staircase that occupied the centre of the hall until he vanished from their sight.

'Don't like that chap,' Jackson murmured half to himself as he followed the inspector towards the rear of the house.

'Neither do I,' the other agreed promptly. 'There's something very odd about him, in my opinion.'

Passing through a door on their left, they found themselves in a large book-lined study. The French windows at the other end opened onto the lawn; and from where he stood gazing out meditatively upon the flowerbeds, Inspector Kennedy turned to greet them. 'Inspector Kennedy — Mr. Jackson,' Charteris introduced them, waving a hand in the direction of the former. 'It was at his suggestion that the Yard was called in.'

'Extreme modesty on your part, wasn't it, Inspector?' Jackson commented with a smile.

But the pleasant-looking man in uniform shook his head deprecatingly. 'Not at all, sir,' he said in a short clipped fashion that contrasted well with the slow, measured enunciation of the Yard man. 'You see, it's the first time we've ever had a murder round here. That is,' he corrected himself hastily, 'since I've been in the vicinity, anyway; so it seemed a good opportunity for studying the Yard methods at close quarters, so to speak.'

'That's a very nice way of putting it. I only hope my old friend here comes up to your expectations, that's all!' remarked Jackson in defiance of a venomous look from Charteris. 'And now, if it's not asking too much, perhaps you wouldn't mind giving me a few details of how my uncle came to meet his death?'

'Of course we will,' Charteris assented willingly, only too pleased that the conversation had taken a less personal turn. 'Sit down, Jaggers.'

As Jackson complied, the inspector stole a glance at Kennedy, who was looking rather surprised at what he obviously considered these most irregular proceedings.

'It's all right, Kennedy,' he reassured him lightly. 'Mr. Jackson's a private crime investigator, and has assisted the Yard — unofficially, of course — upon numerous occasions. Go ahead and tell him all about it.'

'With pleasure.' Well satisfied with this explanation, Kennedy turned to Jackson, who, having lit a cigarette and settled himself in one of the most comfortable chairs he could find, was regarding him drowsily through a haze of tobacco smoke as though he were just about to listen in to the weather report or the fat stock prices over the radio. Overcoming a slight feeling of irritation which this apparent lack of interest inspired in him, the local man began to narrate in his clear, concise way the incidents that had led up to his decision to persuade the chief constable of Hamlin Hollow to summon the aid of Scotland Yard, without more ado.

'It must have been about half-past twelve when I was awakened by a phone call from the station telling me that Sir James Gleeson had been found strangled to death in his study, out at the manor,' he began. 'I dressed quickly, and at a few minutes after one I arrived here, accompanied by a couple of constables and the police surgeon. We found Sir James lying over there.' He pointed to the hearthrug. 'He was stone dead; had been for roughly an hour. The door — ' He indicated that by which they had entered. ' — had one of its panels broken in. You can see that the woodwork above the lock was only put in this morning.'

Jackson glanced at it and saw that this was so.

'The room was much as you see it now — except, of course, that the curtains were drawn and the wall lights on. All the inhabitants of the place were here, including the servants, who were clustered together in the hall. Lady Gertrude, the deceased's second wife, was here. And with her was her step-daughter and Sir James's brother. It was the former who had been responsible for calling up the station.

'I questioned them all; and their answers tallied perfectly. It appeared that the party had broken up for the night at eleven o'clock, at which hour Sir James had announced his intention of retiring to bed. In fact, his wife and daughter actually saw him enter his bedroom. Perhaps I should explain here that Sir James and Lady Gertrude didn't sleep in the same room.

'At a few minutes past twelve, the whole household was aroused by a dreadful scream, which issued from this room. Rushing downstairs as quickly as possible, they found that the door was locked from the inside. Not a sound came from within, yet they were all nevertheless convinced that their sense of direction had not deceived them. Eventually, after a little altercation, Rogers, the butler, and Mr. Burke, one of the guests, broke in a panel and forced an entrance. They found Sir James lying in the same position as we did when we arrived later. He was already dead.' At this point the inspector paused for a moment to clear his throat before proceeding.

'And how did they account for the fact that the murderer was not still in the room?' Jackson put in mildly from behind his smokescreen. 'I take it that he was not, for had he been there would be no mystery to solve.'

'No, sir, he was not. But one of the guests had found the solution to that little problem before I got here. A broken catch to the French windows explained all that away.'

'And who, may I ask, was the sagacious guest to discover that?'

'A gentleman by the name of — ' Here Kennedy consulted his notebook. 'Fritz Hoffman, sir.'

'The famous pianist?'

'Yes, sir. So I was told.'

'Whew!

'As Mr. Hoffman swore he'd not touched the catch,' the inspector continued, undaunted by this interruption, 'I immediately called in the expert from Canterbury and had it tested for fingerprints. But whoever the murderer was, he or she must have used gloves; for he found nothing conclusive on either the catch, the electric light switch or the lamp.'

'So you tested all those, did you, Inspector? And why did you do that?' Jackson broke in on him again with another query.

'Because,' explained the inspector patiently, 'when they broke into this room, all of them swore it was in darkness; and Rogers said he switched the light on from the door. So I figured that unless Sir James was in the act of leaving the room when he was attacked, having extinguished them himself, then somebody else must have done it for him, it being extremely unlikely that he'd be sitting here in the dark.'

'Quite so, Inspector. I see your point.'

'Footprints, of course, were hopeless,' declared Inspector Charteris, taking up the narrative at this point.

'And have you any theory as to who did it, Charteris?' Jackson enquired, lighting a fresh cigarette from the stump of the old one and shifting himself into a more comfortable position.

The big man reddened. 'I don't know that I have yet,' he spluttered awkwardly. 'I've been over the ground thoroughly with Kennedy, of course. And I've questioned the guests and the servants. The only point I've made up my mind upon is that I'm sure it was an inside job.'

'What makes you so sure of that?'

For answer, the inspector rose to his feet and crossed over to the French windows. With two swift movements he drew the curtains, and the room was at once plunged into darkness. The next second he opened them again, and it was once more suffused with the mellow evening sunshine.

'You see,' he explained, returning to his seat, 'even if Sir James had kept all the lights in this room on, they would not have been visible from outside with the curtains drawn. And they *were* drawn, according to all the witnesses. So the intruder, had he been an outsider and unfamiliar with the workings of the establishment, would have naturally assumed that Sir James was in bed, and consequently made the bedroom his direct objective.'

'True. But haven't you overlooked one possibility?' Jackson hinted. 'Granting all you've said, might not the intruder have thought the French windows the easiest way of forcing an entrance?'

'And come upon his victim unexpectedly? Is that what you mean?' the inspector enquired tentatively, and Jackson nodded. 'Ye-es,' he muttered doubtfully, 'but I'm still in favour of it having been somebody inside, all the same.'

'Well, you're possibly quite right,' Jackson conceded. 'But taking it for granted that it happened all as you've said, I don't see how the murderer contrived to join the others immediately afterwards. For according to what Inspector Kennedy has just told us, everybody was present at the time when the body was discovered.'

'I took it that the murderer slipped downstairs after Sir James,' Kennedy broke in, 'but was not sufficiently swift to prevent the door being locked upon him. So finding himself in the passage, he hit upon the idea of creeping out by the back door. It was quite a simple matter then to force the French windows open, commit the murder, and return by the way he'd come, joining the others in the hall.'

'Without any of them noticing that he'd not come from the stairs? It's a possibility, of course. But if it actually happened, it can only have been by a piece of sheer luck that he escaped detection.'

'Don't forget the whole household was in a state of uproar,' Charteris reminded him.

'I'm not forgetting it,' Jackson retorted slowly. 'But even then, it still leaves a great deal to be desired. Anyway, let's pass over it for the moment and go on to something else. Tell me what ideas you've formed concerning a motive?'

The last question was addressed directly to Inspector Charteris, and by way of reply he shook his head dolefully. 'None,' he admitted frankly. 'So far as I can judge, the deceased seemed to have been popular with everybody. All the guests got on well with him. And only a few hours before he died, he announced his daughter's engagement to Mr. Burke.'

'So Joan was engaged, was she?' Jackson smiled to himself as he recalled the last occasion upon which he'd seen her, when she was on vacation, soon after her mother's death. A typically gawky schoolgirl she had appeared to him then, but with a few not inconsiderable claims to prettiness that had in all probability blossomed with the years.

'Didn't Sir James show any signs of tension during the evening?' he asked suddenly.

Charteris shot him a curious look. 'Yes, apparently he did. But had you any particular reason for asking that?'

'I'll tell you.' Briefly he outlined to the two inspectors the contents of the letter he'd received, and how he'd reached his conviction of its having been steamed open. As he told them this, a sudden idea struck him; and he crossed to the wastepaper basket, which stood beside the desk. Dropping onto one knee, he began to rummage about among its contents. And soon he came upon what he was looking for: his telegram of acceptance, which had arrived only on the previous afternoon. Holding the crushed envelope up to the light, he gave a sigh of satisfaction and turned back to Inspector Charteris, who had been watching these operations with an expression of mute bewilderment.

'I'm inclined to agree with you in your theory that this was an inside job, after all!' he declared excitedly. 'This envelope appears to have been steamed open as well.'

'And what does that prove?' inquired the inspector dully.

'Why, don't you see?' Jackson laughed at him. 'It shows the chances are ten to one that Uncle James's letter to me was opened here, before it ever left the house; which proves conclusively that some inside influence has been at work, all along!'

'Of course it does!' Kennedy exploded enthusiastically.

'If that's so, perhaps the butler would

be able to help us?' Charteris suggested meekly.

As though in answer, there came a gentle rap at the door, and the next moment Rogers appeared on the threshold. Crossing the floor swiftly with his catlike tread, he addressed himself to Jackson. 'Lady Gertrude asks you to excuse her, sir,' he said in his obsequious tones, 'and says she hopes you will make yourself comfortable.'

'Thank you, Rogers.'

As the man turned to go, Charteris called him back. 'If you've a moment to spare, Rogers,' he began tactfully, 'I should like to ask you one or two questions.'

'Certainly, sir.' The butler returned to the centre of the room. But for all the suave servility of his voice, Jackson was quick to detect a slight narrowing of the eyes, which gave him the appearance of a hunted animal with its back to the wall.

'It's about a letter,' Charteris continued casually, 'which was dispatched on . . . ' He looked questioningly towards Jackson.

'Saturday.'

'Saturday. Do you remember, by any chance, being entrusted with a letter on that particular day?'

'Yes, I do, sir,' the man replied without hesitation. 'Sir James handed me a letter for the post on Saturday evening. He told me it was very important, and that I was to attend to it myself.'

'And did you?'

'Yes, sir.'

'Hm! I suppose you didn't let it out of your possession between the time Sir James gave it to you and when you put it into the letterbox?'

For a second the man paused, and the narrowing of his eyes became more apparent than ever. 'Now I come to think of it, I believe I did leave it on the hall stand for a few minutes, sir, while I went downstairs to get my umbrella. You see, it rained very heavily down here on Saturday night, as Inspector Kennedy will tell you.'

'It certainly did,' Kennedy corroborated gruffly. 'And that was the only occasion upon which the letter left your possession?'

36

'Yes, sir.' The man's tone was quite definite upon this point.

'You've said you only left it for a few minutes?'

'Yes, sir. Not more than five, at the outside.'

'I see. Now there was a telegram that arrived yesterday afternoon; have you any recollection of this?'

'Yes, sir. It came while Sir James was out. I put it on his desk for him to see when he returned.'

'When did he return?'

'I don't rightly know, sir. I saw nothing of him until just before dinner, when he went upstairs to dress. I remember thinking at the time that he'd left it rather late, especially as he always dressed himself, having a rooted objection to the idea of keeping a valet.'

'All right, Rogers. That'll do.'

With studied unobtrusiveness, the man slipped from the room.

'I still don't like him,' Jackson announced as soon as he'd gone.

'I'm positive he was lying about the letter, anyway,' growled Charteris. 'Five minutes wasn't long enough to complete a job like that! I suppose he thought by admitting he'd left it in the hall, he was establishing an alibi for himself. I'll bet he's in this business up to his neck; but for all that, there's no connecting him with the murder.'

'Why not?' Jackson demanded sharply.

'For the simple reason,' the Yard man pointed out a trifle heavily, 'that the scream happened to be so loud that it roused the servants who sleep at the top of the house, with the result that they came down in a body to investigate — led by our friend Rogers! If he committed the murder and managed to get back to the top floor again in time to hear his victim's scream, he must have been something in the nature of a superman.'

Jackson smiled and gave his companion a playful dig in the ribs.

'Sorry,' he apologised. 'But I'd clean forgotten about the servants; and anyhow, this is the first time I'd heard that Rogers acted as their leader.'

'Hm! Well, he did! And several of them saw him coming out of his room, too. All the staff have their bedrooms up there except the gardener, and he lives in that little cottage I'd just come out of when you saw me this afternoon. He knew nothing, either; said he was out taking his dog for a final airing before turning in, when he heard the scream and started to run in the direction whence it had come. Unfortunately, though, he slipped and twisted his ankle. The poor old chap's been laid up with it all day. That doesn't help us much, does it?'

'Not much,' Jackson agreed despondently. Then suddenly he banged his fist down upon the table. 'Damn it all!' he burst out. 'The key to the whole thing must be somewhere in this house, mustn't it? That being so, it's our job to find it!'

'*Our* job!' echoed Charteris, regarding him with a quizzical smile. 'You don't mean to say you've any intention of mixing yourself up in this troublesome business, Jaggers?'

'I've every intention of mixing myself up in it,' the other retorted hotly. 'What on earth do you think I've been asking you so many questions for?'

But before the inspector had time to answer, the dinner gong unexpectedly boomed forth its dull reverberations, close at hand. And for once it served two purposes, besides its fundamental one of summoning the inmates to the dining-room: it caused a break in the conversation, and at the same time provided a suitable distraction during which the grateful smile that transformed Inspector Charteris's face passed unnoticed.

4

Motive

Joan Gleeson gave the finishing touches to her hair and surveyed herself critically in the long mirror. Considering her recent bereavement, she looked wonderfully fit. Only a vague suggestion of redness about the eyes and an undeniable pallor which all the artifices of a careful make-up were powerless to disguise hinted at a sleepless night and a sad, harassed day.

Next to her mother, who died when she was very young, she had been fonder of her father than of anybody else in the world, despite the fact that he had always been withdrawn from her. It was no personal discredit to her that this was so, for he behaved the same with everybody, preferring to live in his land of lost hopes, peopled with unpleasant stinging regrets, forever reminding him of what, had he played his cards more wisely, he might

41

have made himself.

On his death, Gleeson Manor and all it contained passed to her stepmother; an eventuality he had discussed frequently and unreservedly upon almost every occasion when Lady Gertrude had put into words something of the deep affection she felt for this beautiful home of his ancestors. And now, without the least warning, his hour had struck, and the transference was taking place, sooner than had been expected.

Glancing idly out of the window beside her, Joan's eyes fell upon Jackson's Alvis, where it stood in all its shining magnificence at the foot of the steps. This happened to be the first indication she received of his arrival, for at the time when he was actually making his way up the broad drive, her melancholy thoughts were elsewhere. For a few seconds she gazed at it in mild astonishment; and then, dimly at first, she began to recall something her father had mentioned at dinner last night about Cousin Jaggers coming down for the weekend. Having arrived thus far, and remembering that he was fantastically wealthy, the presence of the super sports car became at once self-explanatory.

Turning back to her mirror again, she dwelt once more upon her reflection — this time albeit even more critically than before. And such wayward things are thoughts that she could not but feel a rebel impulse of gratitude towards her dead father, who had decreed that none of those left behind him should observe the time-honoured custom of mourning.

No sooner did she become conscious of this than she sought to banish it as something unworthy; although was it not in reality a perfectly natural thought? Her father had died, it was true; but life must go on. Besides which, she had not seen Cousin Jaggers since her schooldays, so was it very unpardonably vain on her part that she should wish to impress him favourably?

Turning from her dressing-table, she rose and crossed to the door; and as she did so, the dinner gong sounded. It was by pure coincidence that she chose the same moment to descend the stairs as

Jackson and Charteris did to return from the front door where they had been parting from Kennedy, who was returning to the station; and thus it happened that she and her cousin came face to face.

For his part, he stood as though spellbound, gazing in unaffected admiration at this exquisite woman of nineteen. And with her golden hair, clear blue eyes and smooth skin, she was sufficiently radiant to hold even the most blasé male entranced. Add to all these charms a sensitive and delicately shaped mouth, and you would still have a vastly inadequate portrait of the breath-taking loveliness of the woman who in that brief moment performed the hitherto unparalleled feat of rendering Conway Jackson speechless.

The first to break the silence was Joan herself, as she came down the few remaining stairs and advanced towards him with outstretched hands. 'Why, it's Cousin Jaggers! I don't expect you remember me, do you?'

Almost reverently he took the well-shaped hands in his, and murmured a few words of consolation. 'Of course I remember you, my dear,' he said at last, in answer to her question. 'But you've changed, and become, if I may say so, even more beautiful than I ever thought you would.'

A tidal wave of soft pink swept over her face; and at the same moment, a young man opened the door of the lounge, crossing the hall to join them. The expression of delight that immediately lit up her features at the sight of him told its own story, and rendered the following introduction superfluous.

'This is Mr. Burke,' she said, slipping one arm lightly through his. 'I want you to meet Cousin Jaggers.'

The pleasant-looking red-headed Irishman took his hand in a firm grip. 'How do you do?' he greeted him shortly.

'So you're Joan's fiancé,' Jackson murmured with a smile.

The young man looked surprised. 'How did you find that out?' he asked.

'Elementary, my dear Watson. My friend Inspector Charteris told me. And even if he hadn't, I fancy I should have guessed it the moment I saw you together. Some things are unmistakable.'

'Why, have you met the inspector before, then?' queried Joan in an attempt to lead the conversation away from a topic that bade fair to become rather embarrassing.

'We've met upon several occasions.'

'You see, Miss Gleeson,' Charteris explained, 'for some reason or other, criminology happens to be the only thing that really interests him.'

'True,' Jackson admitted. 'The inspector and I have worked out many cases together, haven't we, Charteris?'

The inspector nodded solemnly. 'We have.'

'Well, don't look so gloomy about it, or they'll get the wrong idea!'

'You're not thinking of helping with this one by any chance, are you?' enquired Pat Burke.

'Yes, are you?' Joan added eagerly. For a fraction of a second, Jackson paused for consideration. Inconceivable though it seemed that either of these charming young people could have anything to do with the recent tragedy, he was not about to take any risks by putting them on their guard. 'Well, that all depends,' he replied cautiously.

'On what?' demanded Joan, showing greater tenacity than he would have credited her with.

'On whether I can be of any use, of course.' And then abruptly changing the subject: 'I say, would you think it awfully rude of me if I were to suggest that we go in to dinner? I'm simply ravenous.'

'Of course not. How rude of us,' she apologised as she led him penitently towards the dining-room.

But even the fact that he had entered that large oak-panelled apartment did not necessarily mean that he was about to partake of the excellent fare he saw spread out upon the long table before him, for there were still further formalities to be observed. These took the shape of introductions to his fellow guests, and they proved sufficiently interesting to make him forget all about the food, although he was quite genuinely hungry.

The first person to be presented to him

was the dead man's brother, Frederick Gleeson, who for some reason he could not remember having seen before. The impression this meeting created in him was a far from pleasant one, the Gleeson cast of countenance being all the rather unprepossessing individual possessed, either physically or mentally, to show that he belonged to that reputable old family at all. A heavy sensualist in his time, and a heavy drinker too, thought Jackson. And he was right: for those two vices had been the only pleasures in the whole of the man's completely aimless life, and in recent years he had been compelled to sacrifice the former to the latter, with the inevitable result that he was now very seldom sober.

The person Jackson was really eager to meet, however, appeared to be absent; so at last, unable to control his curiosity any longer, he enquired after him: 'I thought Fritz Hoffman was staying with you? Isn't he coming in to dinner?'

The name of the famous pianist produced an extraordinary effect upon the robust young Irishman at his elbow, his features losing on the instant all their natural warmth and becoming strangely cold and detached; a transformation Jackson noted with interest.

'Oh yes, he's staying here,' Joan answered him casually, 'but he comes and goes as he sees fit. You see, he's here on holiday before his world tour next month. So Daddy — ' Her voice trembled a little, and Pat Burke squeezed her hand reassuringly. ' — thought he ought to be allowed complete relaxation.'

'He was going for a walk the last time I saw him,' Charteris chimed in.

'Then I may look forward to meeting him later,' said Jackson rather hurriedly. Was it his imagination, or had Joan's voice sounded a little strained as she replied to his question concerning Hoffman? Instinctively he began to smell a rat; and his sense from that moment onwards became twice as acute.

As they seated themselves around the table — he was on Joan's right, since she was occupying her stepmother's place at the head of the table, during her ladyship's absence — he saw that, besides the one vacant chair opposite him that he had taken as being intended for Fritz Hoffman, there were also two others. So there were yet two more to come, were there? Quite a large party, in fact. But who could they be?

He was not long kept in suspense, for the very next moment a stern-looking woman accompanied by a sturdily built tall boy of about ten years old entered the room. In surprise, his eyes sought Joan's, and she at once made them known to him. 'Oh, Tommy!' she cried, addressing herself to the child. 'This is Mr. Jackson — you've heard us talk about him.'

'How do you do, sir?' the little boy said quietly, offering his hand.

'And this is Miss Harcourt, Tommy's governess, Mr. Jackson.'

With muttered greetings, the two shook hands. Jackson gazed at her intently. He felt sure there was something almost incongruous about her, yet for the life of him he could not make out what it was. The introductions over, they began the meal; although Fritz Hoffman was still missing.

As course followed course, the conversation became more and more desultory. The problem uppermost in all their minds, as might be expected under the circumstances, was the strange killing of their host; yet that was the one subject upon which nobody cared to venture. Throughout the frequent lapses, Jackson seemed the only one to remain unembarrassed; for they presented him with an opportunity of studying those around him without their being aware of it. The majority of them emerged from the test triumphantly. The only two who did not were Frederick Gleeson, who seemed to be in a chronic state of agitation about something throughout the entire meal, and Miss Harcourt. She, he felt, was the real mystery there, if anybody was. And he knew now what it was that had struck him as being so incongruous about her at their first meeting.

Severe of countenance, dressed in dowdy characterless clothes, and wearing a pair of heavy horn-rimmed spectacles, this slim woman of indeterminate age and medium height had for some reason or other recently dyed her hair. It gave the impression that she had suddenly decided to let the dye grow out, for the colour now lay in curious streaks; and the roots, so far as he could judge at such a distance, had already regained their natural colour of dark brown. For all this, however, until a few weeks ago, Miss Harcourt must have been a very dazzling blonde. The more he thought of it, the stranger did it seem that this colourless governess should ever have succumbed to such an artificial aid to beauty. He must find out more about her, he decided.

From herself it would be impossible, all his efforts to draw her out so far having elicited nothing beyond a few monosyllabic retorts, which even he was bound to admit sounded far from encouraging. On the other hand, if he asked any of the others about her, he could scarcely hope to avoid giving himself away. This left only two courses open to him: one, he could seek information from her charge, little Tommy — which in all likelihood would prove a sheer waste of time; or two, he could take a single member of the party into his confidence. The last seemed the most hopeful. But which one?

This was decided for him in a rather novel way. Dinner over, they began slowly wending their way towards the lounge for coffee. By chance, Jackson happened to be one of the last to move, and as he did so he felt a light touch upon his arm. Turning to see who it was, he found himself looking down at Joan.

'Will you come into the garden with me for a few moments?' she asked him softly. 'There's something I want to talk to you about.'

'Of course, Joan.'

Obediently, he followed her into the hall; and from thence through the little doorway at the back of the house, out into the coolness of the garden. By this time the shadows were just beginning to lengthen into twilight, while the first scattered stars twinkled in the vast blue firmament above them.

'Must take a great deal of keeping in order, a garden like this,' Jackson remarked practically, by way of making conversation. 'How many gardeners do you keep?'

'Only one. We have some of the men from the village in to do the heavy work.'

'Good idea. Cigarette?'

'Thanks.' She took one from his proffered case, and he lit it for her in silence.

As they were passing beneath an arbour of roses, she took hold of his arm impulsively. 'You will help us, Cousin Jaggers, won't you?' she implored. 'I know you'll be able to find Daddy's murderer, if you want to!'

Jackson patted her hand lightly. 'I wish it were all as simple as that,' he answered in a kind voice. 'But I'll do my best, I promise you.'

She breathed a sigh of relief. 'Thank you!' she murmured fervently. Then: 'But why didn't you tell me that before?'

He smiled. 'Everybody's under suspicion in a case like this until they're proved innocent, my dear,' he reminded her.

'Of course! How stupid of me! Inspector Charteris said something like that when he asked everybody to stay down here a few days longer in order to help on the investigation.'

'But I'm going to take a chance on it and exonerate you.'

'Why?' she enquired bluntly, looking up at him with her beautiful wide eyes.

'For the simple reason, my dear, that I need some help. And in the absence of Lady Gertrude, you seem the most likely person to give it me.'

At the mention of her stepmother, Joan's features hardened. 'I'm afraid you won't get much assistance from her,' she burst out suddenly. 'But — oh, well, you'll find out for yourself without my telling you.'

'Find out what?' Jackson demanded, immediately on the alert.

'Please don't ask me that,' she pleaded with strange insistency. 'I'll tell you anything else you want to know. Really, I will!'

'Always supposing you know the answers yourself,' he chided her gently. 'Very well, then. You've brought it on yourself; so here goes. Question number one: who in the world is Tommy, and what's he doing down here?'

For the first time during their conversation she smiled, and playfully led him through the shrubbery towards a stone bench where they seated themselves. 'I thought you looked rather surprised when I introduced you to him,' she admitted with a little laugh. 'He's Lady Gertrude's adopted son.'

Jackson emitted a long whistle. 'How damned silly of me!'

'Not at all. How were you to know? It only took place about six weeks ago. Daddy was in London, and I was away on holiday. When we returned, lo and behold, we were greeted by Tommy!'

'Whatever made her do it?'

'I don't know. But she's always wanted a son; and she came across Tommy in Paris.'

'Was she alone?'

'Yes. Why?'

'Oh, nothing. But your family seem to go in for solitary holidays, don't they?'

'I suppose we do. We were always like that, though. Daddy thought it did us all good to get away from each other once a year. But to return to Tommy: he was living out there with some appalling people, Lady Gertrude told us; and so when his drunken father was killed in a car crash, she persuaded the mother to let her adopt him.'

'Well, I suppose she might have done considerably worse for herself. He seems a nice enough kid.'

'He is, as kids go.'

'Don't you like them?'

'Not very much.'

'Don't you ever want to have any of your own?'

Joan dropped her eyes. 'That would be different,' she murmured demurely.

Jackson laughed. 'Now for Miss Harcourt,' he said, returning to business. 'What do you know of her?' But to his disappointment, she only shook her head.

'Nothing,' she admitted truthfully.

'Don't you know even where she came from?'

'Paris, I think. But she was installed here while I was away.'

'Hm! Do you like her?'

'Not very much.'

Jackson overcame his disappointment by turning to a fresh subject. 'And while we're on the topic of likes and dislikes,' he said briskly, 'there's something I've been itching to ask you; something a little personal, I'm afraid.'

'I know,' she said, anticipating his question. 'It's about Fritz. You want to know why Pat and I were so cold about him, don't you?'

Jackson nodded. 'Why were you?'

'It's rather difficult to explain,' she began, showing the first signs of diffidence. 'You see, Fritz was in love with me, and — and Daddy was very anxious that I should marry him.'

'But you didn't want to?'

'Of course I didn't!' The colour flamed in her cheeks as she indignantly denied the suggestion. 'I was in love with Pat. But Fritz won Father over to his side, and that put us against him. He's terribly nice, really. But ever since I turned him down, he's been sort of aloof. But then, that's understandable, I suppose,' she added inconsequentially.

'Quite,' Jackson agreed tacitly.

'Of course, Pat's absurdly jealous of him because of his influence over Daddy. He doesn't mean to be unkind.'

And well he might be jealous, thought Jackson to himself. For what could it be this boy had, that a genius of the calibre of Fritz Hoffman had not? An ageless question, and one he was not disposed to answer at the moment, even if he could. Dismissing it, he rose to his feet. 'Well, I think we'll leave it at that for the moment, shall we?' he suggested easily. 'If I don't bring you back soon, that jealous young man of yours'll be ready to tear my hair out!'

'There's one person who might be of some use to you,' she said brightly a few moments later, when they were retracing their footsteps in the direction of the house. 'Old Ferguson, the gardener. He told me a queer tale this morning about having seen something last night 'too horrible to talk about'. It was because of what he saw that he stumbled and hurt his foot.'

'That's funny,' muttered Jackson. 'Charteris never told me anything about it.'

'He didn't know,' she explained simply. 'Ferguson was afraid people would only laugh at him; and so he made me promise not to tell anybody, not even the police.'

'So you told me instead? That's what I call a nice compromise! I must take the first opportunity I can to visit Mr. Ferguson.'

'You won't give me away to him, will you?'

'Of course not.'

'Thanks.'

By this time they had reached the house, to find that the music room — which like the study led into the garden — was a blaze of light; whilst through the open French windows there floated the mellifluous notes of a piano.

'It must be Fritz,' Joan murmured.

Jackson nodded, for he could have told that touch in a million; besides the fact that he was rendering a quaint little German lullaby of his own composition for which he had become rightly famous.

'He always plays that for Tommy at bedtime,' Joan whispered as they tiptoed together through the windows into the softly lighted room beyond. The scene that greeted them was what they might have expected. The guests, having torn themselves away from the lounge, had arranged their chairs in a wide semicircle and were listening with rapt attention; while beside the piano stood little Tommy, his plump face flushed with pleasure. But the one who drew and held all one's scrutiny was the man himself.

Slim and neat in his perfectly fitting tweed suit, with his thick fair hair gleaming in the light cast by the lamp beside him and his pleasant bearded face adorned with a dreamy smile, he appeared at first sight anything but the conventional idea of a criminal. Yet, as Jackson reminded himself, if what Joan had told him in the garden was true — and he saw no reason to doubt it — this man was the only person present who had, so far as he knew, any motive at all for murdering Sir James Gleeson.

But was fury for the elder man for allowing his daughter to become engaged to Pat Burke really a strong enough motive for murder? It certainly didn't seem like it; although many crimes had been committed, as well he knew, upon far less provocation. Then, in the musician's favour, was the fact that he had drawn Kennedy's attention to the broken catch in the study, before the other discovered it for himself. But might that not have been merely for the purpose of putting himself in well with the forces of justice from the start?

Jackson shook his head in bewilderment. Could those delicate hands, which had given delight to so many countless thousands, have choked the life out of a fellow human being? Surely not.

Keeping these tangled thoughts to himself, he stood quite still, watching, with a curious sort of hypnotic fascination the long flexible fingers as they passed with incredible deftness and subtlety over the ivory keys.

5

' . . . Next Time it Will be You!'

While the last note still hung quivering on the calm night air, Jackson and his fair companion advanced towards the piano. His whispered instructions about keeping their conversation in the garden a secret were answered by an understanding nod from Joan as the pianist rose to greet them.

After the two men had been introduced, and Hoffman had made his excuses for failing to put in an appearance at dinner — he said he had lost himself for two hours on the downs, and indeed would not be with them now had he not been fortunate enough to come across a yokel who directed him — it was well past Tommy's bedtime. And for one so young, Jackson was very impressed with the well-mannered way in which the child bade them all good night. Whoever his parents were, judging by his behaviour, they must have been pretty well bred, so Lady Gertrude's action did not seem nearly so inexplicable, after all!

No sooner had he left them than Miss Harcourt decided it was time for her to retire also; and early though the hour was, nobody succeeded in persuading her to remain: a circumstance that annoyed Jackson very much, for his interest in this strange woman, far from decreasing as the evening wore on, was growing deeper. And with her exit from the music-room, he saw whatever chance he might have had of getting to know her better fading away into thin air.

Leaving Joan in the company of the others, he and Inspector Charteris made their way back to the study. It was plain to see that the latter was longing to hear what information, if any, Jackson had extracted from Joan in the interim. And no sooner had they seated themselves than he asked point blank what had taken place between them.

Keeping nothing back, Jackson gave him a detailed account of the entire interview, and Charteris seized avidly upon the theory that Fritz Hoffman might turn out to be the man they were looking for. Jackson, however, failed to express so much confidence in the idea.

'Charteris,' he replied slowly in answer to the other's rather truculent demand as to what he had against it, 'if I told you, you'd only laugh at me.'

'It'd be the first opportunity you've ever given me, then. The boot's usually been on the other foot,' the big man boomed out, not untruthfully.

'Very well. I'll give you your chance now! Agreed that Hoffman seems to be the only person, so far as we know, who had any motive for murdering Sir James, I still don't believe he did it. And my excuse for not believing it is about the weakest you've ever heard. It's just this: for some reason, he simply doesn't impress me as being a murderer, that's all!' He paused. 'Now have your laugh, Charteris. I deserve it, I know!'

But the inspector did not laugh; instead he looked amazed. 'But Jaggers,' he remonstrated gently, 'you must have a stronger reason than that? You can't dismiss a plausible theory like this one just because the suspect doesn't slink about looking like a figure out of a third-rate melodrama!'

'Sounds crazy, doesn't it? But I'm afraid it's what I'm doing, all the same.'

'Do you suspect anybody else? Is it Miss Harcourt, do you think? You seemed to be very interested in her.'

'I am. I think she knows a great deal more than she's letting on.'

'I agree with you there.'

'But I almost forgot!' Jackson burst out suddenly. 'I must be popping over to see the gardener.'

'To find out what he saw that was 'too horrible to talk about'?' asked Charteris with a slightly scornful smile.

'That's it! He'll possibly tell me, if I use a little tact — being one of the family and all that. Now you walk across with me, like a good chap, and tell me what answers Miss Harcourt gave when you interrogated her, will you?'

'All right. Is it warm enough to go out without a hat?' the inspector enquired, rising to his feet.

'Good Lord, yes!' retorted Jackson, who was by this time standing at the French windows. 'Come on!' he cried, throwing them open.

Together the two men passed through the windows and struck out across the lawn towards the belt of trees. The windows of the music-room were still open, and the light fretted a golden pathway among the shadows clustering in the garden.

During their short stroll, Jackson learned all about Miss Harcourt's supposed movements on the night when one horrified scream had announced to the sleeping inmates of Gleeson Manor that their host was being murdered on the floor below them. In common with the others, she claimed to have been wakened by this, having fallen asleep barely half an hour earlier. Her first thought being for the child, she at once rushed to his room at the front of the house, where she found him sitting up in bed, transfixed with terror at the unexpected sound that had disturbed his slumbers. Seeing the state he was in, she stayed to calm him down by the use of an ingenious explanation that it was his own scream which had awakened him, and had for that matter awakened her also. Apparently the child believed this, for shortly afterwards he fell asleep again. As soon as she felt reasonably sure there was little chance of his reawakening before morning, the governess slipped from the room and joined the others in the study.

'And this, I take it, was immediately prior to Kennedy's arrival?' Jackson interrupted the inspector at this juncture.

'Yes. About a quarter of an hour, according to her own estimate.'

'So she was the only one, with the exception of the child, who was not actually present when Sir James's body was discovered!'

'That's a point, of course,' the inspector admitted. 'Though if she'd done it, she would most likely have made a special effort to be one of the first on the spot, so as to establish an alibi.'

'Was Hoffman there?'

'Yes. He wasn't one of the first, but he

arrived a few minutes after the door had been broken in.'

'Allowing himself sufficient time to run out through the French windows and let himself in by the back door, which he had specially left open for the purpose?' Jackson suggested banteringly.

But the inspector was in no mood for having his leg pulled. 'There *have* been stranger things,' he grumbled. 'After all, we know it was either one of the guests or else somebody in the family, because the servants have all vouched for each other; so that counts them out.'

'Unless some of them were lying.' Charteris gave a grunt of impatience. 'Look here,' he cried irritably, 'I thought you were going to help, not make things more difficult!'

'You wouldn't have me neglect any possibility, would you?'

Having no answer to hand, the inspector contented himself with another grunt. By this time, they had passed through the belt of trees and were standing before the gardener's vine-covered cottage, one window on the ground floor of which was lit up by the kind of mellow light one usually associates with an oil lamp.

'You'd better not come in,' advised Jackson. 'I've a hunch I'll be able to get more out of him by myself.'

'Perhaps you will. The old man seems a little scared of the police,' Charteris agreed, with one of his surprising flashes of tolerance. 'I'll hang about out here for you.' And so saying, he strolled off quietly into the shadows.

Looking after him, Jackson experienced anew that feeling of admiration he had always felt for this clear-sighted official. For how many other Yard men would give him such a free hand? Not many, he guessed.

Seeing there was no knocker, he rapped loudly on the wooden door with his knuckles and waited for a reply. This was not immediately forthcoming; although shuffling footsteps, heard from inside, soon gave him to understand that his summons was being attended to.

At last the door was slowly opened, and he became conscious of two pairs of eyes staring out at him from the gloom. One pair belonged to a white-haired old man and the other to the collie, which crouched obediently at his heels.

'Good evening, Mr. Ferguson. My name's Conway Jackson; Sir James was my uncle. May I come in for a few moments?'

'Certainly, sir,' the man replied civilly enough, and stood aside for him to enter. As he did so, the dog gave a low growl.

'Doesn't like strangers, do you, boy?' Jackson coaxed the animal pleasantly.

'I don't generally have many visitors, sir,' Ferguson explained in his deep, rough voice. 'Bob's not used to it. And that detective chap upset him this afternoon, for a start. I hope you're not one of 'em, are you, sir?'

Jackson laughed. 'Nothing like that about me,' he told the old man reassuringly. 'Where do I go? In here?' He moved towards the lighted room.

'If you will, sir,' said Ferguson, following him painfully with the aid of a stick. 'I'm afraid I'm a bit slow, but you see, I hurt my foot last night.'

'So Miss Gleeson told me. Can I give you a hand?'

71

'No, thank you, sir. I shall be all right.' With the maximum of difficulty, he managed to drag himself into the little sitting-room, where he heaved himself into an armchair, motioning his guest to do likewise; it was then Jackson had an opportunity to study him for the first time.

To call him handsome would have been an exaggeration. But pleasant after a weather-beaten sort of fashion, he most certainly was; and his tousled mop of unruly white hair lent a certain softness to his features, which might otherwise have erred on the side of harshness. The dog sat on its haunches beside him, and its great saucer eyes never left Jackson's face for a fraction of a second. From time to time the man patted it lightly with his dark gnarled hand, the gesture being mutely expressive of his devotion.

'Well, sir, and what is it you're wanting of a poor old man like me?' he enquired; and Jackson thanked him silently for breaking the ice.

'Nothing very much, Mr. Ferguson. It's like this. I've been asked by Miss Gleeson to undertake a little private investigation into how Sir James came to meet his death. It's strictly *private*, mind you,' he repeated, underlining the word, as he observed the first flicker of hostility in the old man's eyes. 'And since nobody seems able to throw any light upon the business, I thought maybe you might be able to help me.'

He came to an abrupt full stop and waited for the gardener to say something; which he did, but only after a weighty pause. 'And what, if it's not an impertinence to ask, sir, made you think that?' he queried.

'The fact that being outside the house at the time, I thought you might have seen something while you were walking about in the grounds.'

'What sort of thing should I be expected to see at that time of night?' the old man persisted, eyeing him suspiciously.

'I've really no idea, Mr. Ferguson,' Jackson admitted frankly. 'But supposing, by any chance, you had noticed something, I'd be most tremendously grateful if you'd tell me about it. You see, though it may appear unimportant, at this juncture there's no knowing where a clue, however slight, may lead us to eventually; especially at the moment, when we have so little to go upon.'

At this admission, the man looked up. 'D'you mean the police aren't getting on with it as quickly as they should, sir?' he asked sharply.

'Well, they can hardly be expected to if people withhold information, can they?'

'Is that what you think I've been doing, sir?' A momentary gleam of defiance appeared in his dark eyes.

Jackson hastened to put him at his ease. 'Of course not,' he assured him hurriedly. 'I only wanted to hear your story from your own lips, instead of relying upon what I can gather second hand, that's all.'

'I see.' The gleam of defiance died down, and the conversation began to take a more intimate turn. 'To tell you the truth, sir,' confessed the man, leaning forward in his chair, 'I'm afraid I *did* keep something back when that inspector came to question me this afternoon — but it was only because I was afraid he'd think me crazy if I told him. I'm as keen as anybody to see Sir James's murderer brought to justice. Sir James was a good master to me, and I'm not likely to forget it.'

'I'm sure you're not,' Jackson agreed soothingly. 'He was a good uncle to me, and I'm not likely to forget that either.'

The man leaned even closer. 'Seeing that's the case, and you're one of the family,' he whispered, his voice becoming almost inaudible in its intensity, 'I'll take the risk of your thinking me crazy, and tell you what it was I saw. For I did see something, sir, and I shall remember it till my dying day!'

Jackson began to experience an odd tingling sensation at the base of his spine as the old white-haired gardener proceeded to recount, in tones of superstitious awe, his experience of the previous night. 'I was a bit restless last night, sir,' he started, 'and so was Bob. I could hear him twisting and turning about in his kennel outside; so, getting out of bed, I dressed myself with the idea of taking him for a brisk walk round the grounds. It was a hot night, so I thought it'd do us both good.

'I never chain him up, and I only had to whistle for him to come bounding to my side. And so we set off across the lawn. The clock down in Hamlin Hollow had just struck twelve, and I was walking along smoking my pipe, all peaceful like, when all of a sudden I heard a scream. I stopped dead in my tracks, and so did Bob. Then, having made up our minds where it'd come from, we both started running towards the house, as fast as we could go.

'We got through the trees all right, and were just racing across the lawn when I saw something that froze the blood in my veins. Coming out of the study window was a black shape. It wasn't like anything human, sir, man or woman — it was like some horrible sort of animal! All doubled up it was, and ran close to the ground. I couldn't see its face, and I'm not even sure it had one. Taking a good hold of myself, I put on an extra spurt; but luck was against me, and I must have stumbled over something, for the next thing I knew I was stretched out full length on the ground, with Bob standing over me, growling for all he was worth.'

'And the shape?'

'I don't know, sir. When I looked up it had vanished — as though it had never been!'

'What did you do, then?'

'Went over to the house and stayed there until the police came. Inspector Kennedy soon saw I was in too much pain to answer any questions just then, so he let one of the constables help me back here.'

'And you've no idea where the shape went to, after you saw it coming out of the study?'

'None, sir. I only wish I had; for whatever it was, I'd take my life on it that it killed Sir James!'

'You know, I'm rather inclined to agree with you,' retorted Jackson drily.

Soon after this, he rose to go. And having thanked Ferguson for his co-operation and begged him not to disturb himself, found his way out.

He had not taken more than half a dozen paces before the inspector stepped out of the shadows and fell into stride beside him. Briefly, without waiting to be asked, Jackson repeated what he had just learned. Charteris listened in silence; so far as he was concerned, it could be easily fitted in with the existing theory about Hoffman. As Jackson realised this, he felt a vague twinge of resentment, and relapsed into a moody silence which lasted until they were within sight of the house.

'Fine place for a child to be in, I must say!' Charteris grunted, apropos of nothing in particular.

Jackson agreed wearily. 'Aunt Gertrude ought to send him away,' he commented without interest.

'Why don't you suggest it?' the inspector asked him.

Jackson looked up, startled. 'Why, I haven't even seen her yet, have I?' he said irritably. 'In fact, I'd almost forgotten about her until you reminded me. I suppose she'll see me some time tonight.'

'Suppose so.'

These last words carried them into the study, through the French windows, which stood open as they'd left them.

'I say, I feel awfully sticky; I think I'll bathe my face and hands,' declared Jackson, turning to his companion. 'Where's the bathroom?'

Charteris gave him a few terse directions; and having promised that he'd only be gone a few minutes, he passed out into the hall and up the broad staircase on to the first floor.

He soon found the bathroom; and the coolness of the water did much towards alleviating the hot clamminess that was in his head.

Feeling considerably better, he turned out the light, and was just making his way back along the passage when he came to an abrupt standstill. The sound of voices raised in anger had penetrated to him from an adjacent room on his left. By nature, he was anything but an eavesdropper; but one of those voices happened to be a woman's, and it sounded strangely familiar.

In an effort to tear himself away, he took two or three paces towards the head of the stairs. But this time something stronger than mere curiosity detained him; for down that quiet hall came floating words that were as momentous as they were menacing!

'Go away before it's too late,' a woman's voice enunciated in low, vibrant tones. 'Go away, you fool — next time it will be you!'

Jackson was by this time standing directly outside the door, behind which the conversation was taking place; but even he, nimble though he was, was not quick enough to jump out of the way when it flew unexpectedly open. Without any warning, he found himself gazing into a pair of blazing eyes set in a countenance of extreme pallor.

'Mr Jackson!' cried a hard, ominous voice.

Without taking his eyes off the face before him, Jackson gave a slight bow. So, after all, he reflected grimly, he had been destined to meet Lady Gertrude even sooner than he'd expected!

6

Out of the Darkness

At that moment, the person to whom Lady Gertrude had been talking decided to beat a hasty retreat; and a very clumsy sort of affair it turned out to be. Frederick Gleeson, for it was he, sidled awkwardly out of the room, and once beyond the protection of his sister-in-law's broad shoulders, made for the stairs like a frightened hare.

'Come inside,' invited Lady Gertrude when he had gone.

But there was no ring of cordiality in her tones; and as Jackson followed her in, he felt completely lost as to what would be his best method of approach. To pretend he'd heard nothing of their conversation would sound utterly unconvincing; while if he owned up to having heard it, he would have to face the inevitable accusation of eavesdropping.

Without asking him to be seated, she closed the door and stood facing him. 'And since when have you numbered spying among your accomplishments?' she demanded harshly.

So it had come! Looking into her curiously stony eyes, he made his excuses.

'So you see, Aunt Gertrude,' he ended up lamely, 'it was only by the merest chance that I happened to be outside at all.'

Whether she believed him or not, it was impossible to say, her next remark proving no lead in that direction.

'You're interested in criminology, I believe?'

'Yes, I am.'

'And I suppose you're thinking of getting yourself mixed up in this case?'

She repeated the question when he failed to reply at once.

'That is something I should prefer not to answer, if it's all the same to you, Aunt Gertrude.'

'Which means you are. What you heard just now must have aroused your curiosity?'

'It would be pointless to deny that.'

She took a few steps nearer to him. 'How much did you hear?' she demanded imperiously. But in odd contrast to her authoritative bearing, he noted a look very akin to fear lingering in the depths of her shadowy eyes.

'I've told you already — ' he began, when she cut him short.

'That you only heard my last sentence. But is that the truth? Will you swear to it?'

'Certainly, if you wish me to.'

'What did you make of it?'

'I don't quite know,' Jackson admitted candidly. 'I was hoping,' he added with caution, 'that when you asked me to come in just now, it was with the intention of explaining it to me.'

'And can you give me one good reason why I should?'

'Yes. I can give you one, precisely: I take it you wish your husband's murderer to be brought to justice?'

His quick eye perceived a slight tremor.

'What has that to do with it?' she asked a trifle unsteadily.

'Only this: if you truly wish to see your

husband's murderer brought to justice, you will not suppress any information that might prove of assistance to the police in their search for him.'

'The police or you?' she cut in sharply, all trace of her former nervousness having vanished completely.

Determined to avoid being tricked into any direct admission, he fenced with her skilfully.

'Whichever you prefer,' he replied. 'Though I should advise you to tell me; then I can use my discretion as to whether I hand it on or keep it to myself.'

'I see,' she retorted with a sneer. 'And if I refuse to tell either of you? What can you do then?'

'Nothing. I can only appeal to your better nature.'

Here, she laughed outright; and it was not a pleasant sound. 'Better nature!' she mocked. 'Do you mean to say you still believe in that sort of rubbish? My poor boy! And I thought you'd grown up!'

'Grown up or not,' he countered quietly, 'I'm still idealistic enough to believe you loved my uncle.'

The shaft, drawn at random, went straight to its mark; and he had the satisfaction of seeing the woman before him wince for the first time.

'You're right to believe it,' she murmured. 'I did love him. I may not have shown it always, because I'm not a demonstrative kind of woman; but I loved him as much as he did me. And if you remember anything about your uncle, you'll know that was a great deal.'

'I do remember.'

He remembered a number of other things too! For example, the first time he had met his aunt. He recalled distinctly, even now, how impressed he had been by her cold, statuesque beauty; and how delighted and surprised at the unexpected warmth of her smile. That smile he had always looked upon as an external demonstration of her feelings for his uncle, who, although he had made her his second wife when he was well advanced in years, had nevertheless retained sufficient of the fire of younger days to worship the very ground she walked upon.

Looking at her now, he could not help

comparing this handsome, regal woman with the beautiful carefree creature he had known in his youth. Even then she'd had her trials to bear, though, for the Gleeson family were very conservative and old-fashioned in their principles, and the fact that she'd been married before — a subject upon which she observed the most curious reticence, even refusing to disclose his name — and came to Sir James completely penniless, was commented upon by them with a full measure of cattiness.

'And because of that, I hope you're going to tell me what it was you were talking about.'

His words were followed by a long silence, during which both the occupants of Lady Gertrude's boudoir experienced a variety of emotions.

For the first few seconds of this, Jackson felt quite convinced that he had succeeded in breaking down her defences. But he was speedily disillusioned.

'Supposing I told you that what you overheard me saying a few minutes ago could have no connection with my husband's death; would that satisfy you? It'll have to,' she continued, without allowing him time to answer, 'because it's all the explanation I intend to give you.'

'In that case, there's nothing left for me to say,' Jackson replied politely, moving towards the door.

'I'm glad you realise that. But one thing more, before you go! Let me warn you not to waste your time in questioning my brother-in-law; for, believe me, he will tell you nothing.'

'Thanks for the advice, Aunt Gertrude.' He turned, suddenly remembering something. 'Oh, by the way, I suppose there's no objection to my staying the night?'

'No objection in the world. But unfortunately all the bedrooms happen to be occupied. I'm so sorry.'

Checking the angry retort that rose to his lips, Jackson left the room, closing the door behind him. Hardly had he done so when he heard the key turning in the lock.

As he continued on his interrupted way towards the head of the stairs, he felt himself assailed by a strong wave of depression — fostered, no doubt, by the knowledge that in the last few minutes when he had hoped to learn something of his mysterious aunt, he had failed dismally. He could have kicked himself out of sheer annoyance.

In the hall, he encountered the inspector. 'Hullo, I was beginning to wonder where you'd got to,' he hailed Jackson cheerfully. 'What happened? Did you lose yourself?'

'Far from it,' Jackson retorted bitterly. 'I've been having a talk with my aunt.'

'Oh?'

The two men made their way back to the study, where without pausing to reply to the inspector's query, Jackson crossed over to the large roll-topped desk by the window. For some time he rummaged around, apparently looking for something. At last, having failed to discover what he wanted, he turned to Charteris. 'Where's the phone directory?' he asked.

'In there,' replied the inspector, pointing to the centre drawer. 'But who on earth do you want to ring up at this time of night?'

Without answering, Jackson looked up something in the book, which he placed on the desk, and moved the telephone towards him. Lifting the receiver, he gave a local number, at which the quizzical expression on the inspector's face deepened. Before he had time to say anything about it, however, Jackson was through.

'Hello . . . the Kentish Arms?' he enquired. 'Is that Judy? This is Jaggers speaking. Remember? Good . . . What? Oh, not at all. Of course you didn't like to tell me . . . Listen; I want you to reserve a room for me . . . yes . . . I'll be down in about half an hour . . . Supper? Yes, I'd love some . . . Right. I'll be seeing you in half an hour then . . . Goodbye.' He replaced the receiver, and sinking into the swivel chair, turned to Charteris again. 'You will have gathered from that, that the hospitality of Gleeson Manor has not been extended to me for tonight,' he announced crisply.

'So I see,' the inspector replied. Then he gave a wicked chuckle. 'I see also that you're on very good terms with the barmaid at the Kentish Arms,' he pronounced with an air of heavy playfulness. 'How did you manage that, on so short an acquaintance?'

'Technique, my boy, that's all,' Jackson retorted. 'Come over some day, and I'll give you a lesson.'

The older man chortled delightedly. Then he suddenly became serious. 'But, all fooling apart, why aren't you staying the night? There must be plenty of room.'

'Not according to my aunt.'

'Did she absolutely refuse to let you stay?'

'She did. Point blank.'

'But what for?'

'Scared of what I might find out, possibly; or am I being too conceited?'

'Not at all. Tell me about it.'

And without any omission, however slight, Jackson told him the entire sequence that had taken place upstairs.

When he had finished, Charteris gave a gasp of surprise. 'But what — what an — ' he spluttered incoherently. 'What an incredible thing!'

'That's what I thought,' the other agreed caustically.

''Next time it will be you', the inspector repeated to himself. 'Do you suppose she was referring to the murder of Sir James?'

'Looks like it, doesn't it?'

'She was apparently quite sure we'd get nothing out of her brother-in-law. I wonder if she was right, though?'

'Offhand, I'm inclined to think she was.'

'Why?' Charteris demanded.

'Because his whole attitude, so far as I could judge anyway, seemed to be one of cringing nervousness. If you ask me, I think he's carrying his life in his hands, and wouldn't dare to tell us anything, even if he could.'

But in this last estimate he wronged Frederick Gleeson, as he was to discover in the near future.

'Would it do any harm to have him in and question him, do you think?'

'Frankly, I do. It'd be putting him on his guard. Better to watch, and wait for him to make a slip.'

'Supposing he doesn't, though?'

'Hm! It might be a long wait.'

'Somehow I don't think it will be. Aunt Gertrude's threat leads us to believe that the murderer is still on the premises — a circumstance we've always suspected. It also gives a hint of further outrages. 'Next time' . . . Something tells me there *will* be a next time, and I don't think it's so far off, either!'

'Are you thinking of staying on to see it? Or has her ladyship's refusal to let you sleep in the house damped your enthusiasm?'

'What do you think?'

'I think it's made you keener than ever.'

'And you're right.'

Charteris stretched himself and cleared his throat noisily. 'All the same, I don't enjoy sitting on a time bomb, waiting for it to go off,' he complained. 'It's too damned nerve-wracking for my taste.'

Jackson rose to his feet and crossed to his side, patting him lightly on the shoulder. 'I'm sorry, but I'm afraid it's what you'll have to do, old friend,' he said gently, seating himself on the heavy oak table facing him, and playing absent-mindedly with a pair of spectacles that lay on its polished surface beside the inspector's note-book and pencil. 'And now, one thing more before I go. Would you mind telling me what account my aunt gave of herself when you questioned her? I presume you did question her, by the way?'

'You bet I did,' the inspector affirmed. 'But her answers were exactly the same as the others. She was awakened by the scream and came straight downstairs, found her husband lying dead on the floor, and waited for the arrival of the police.'

'You're sure she said she came straight downstairs, are you?' Jackson asked with a faraway look.

'Quite. She came after her brother-in-law. Why?'

'Oh, nothing much,' Jackson retorted, lazily putting the spectacles on. 'Only, unlike our friend Miss Harcourt, she doesn't seem to have spared a thought for little Tommy, does she?'

'I don't know if we can say that! She might have thought of him, but decided that her husband was of more impor-tance, especially under the peculiar circumstances,' the inspector argued.

'True. But she had every reason to believe her husband was safe in bed. How did she recognise his scream? And why didn't she go to his bedroom?'

'Because she knew the scream came from the study.'

'Perfect sense of direction. Did she go to the child afterwards?'

'No, because Miss Harcourt told her he was asleep.'

'And she took her word for it, without going to see for herself?'

'Yes. Damn it all, what's so funny about that?'

'Only that my aunt seems to have taken the whole affair very calmly.'

'She certainly didn't look distracted about it when I saw her,' the inspector admitted.

Jackson looked at him sharply. 'Did it ever occur to you that she might have been expecting it?'

'It didn't at the time,' the Inspector replied thoughtfully, 'but now you come to mention it, it might quite well have been so.'

'I think the promptness with which she acted definitely points to it,' Jackson continued eagerly. 'And if that's the case, and she knew of it beforehand, she's possibly aware already of what the next move will be.'

'You mean you think she knows the identity of the murderer?'

'More than likely.'

'But what can be her reason for shielding him?'

Jackson slipped from the table and faced the inspector squarely. 'If we knew that, Charteris, we should be well on the road towards solving the whole problem. And now,' he added with a complete change of tone, 'I must be getting on my way.'

'Before you do that, you'd better give me back my spectacles,' growled the inspector, rising also, and holding out his hand.

'These yours?' Jackson asked with a laugh, handing them back to their owner. 'Shocking habit of mine! I never can resist trying on other people's glasses. It's becoming quite a mania!'

'Thanks. I only use them for reading,' Charteris informed him hastily as he snapped them into a case. 'I'm not so young as I used to be, you know.'

'The obvious answer to that being, none of us are. I won't say goodnight to anybody — it might be a little embarrassing, so perhaps you'll do it for me? I take it you're not coming yet awhile?'

'Not for an hour or so. Kennedy's calling for me later, in his car; I'm staying at his place.'

Still conversing, they passed out into the hall.

'The inquest is tomorrow morning. It's in the village hall — next door to the Kentish Arms. Drop in, if you'd care to.'

'What time?'

'Nine o'clock.'

'No, thanks! Nobody tempts little Jaggers out of his comfy bed at that inclement hour. Call for me when it's over, will you?'

'All right, you lazy blighter!'

By this time they were on the porch, and began descending the steps to where the car awaited them. Having settled himself comfortably in the driving seat, Jackson had turned to say something to his companion when the words became frozen upon his lips.

Out of the blackness came a chuckle, so soft and eerie that the two men shuddered involuntarily.

'Good God!' murmured the inspector fervently, thereby voicing what they both felt. For a sound of such insane malevolence could scarcely have been made by anything human.

7

An Unexpected Visitor

All the way down to the Kentish Arms, Jackson was pursued by that laugh. It came to him in the faint rustling of the trees, in the agitated scampering of a rabbit into its hole, in the crunching of his own wheels on the country road. And each time he rounded a corner — the road ran tortuously, twisting first one way and then another, until it reached the comparative peace of Hamlin Hollow — he half-expected to see something, he didn't know what, but something revolting, to account for that haunting sound.

Had he encountered the features of some hideous gargoyle sticking out between the trim hedgerows, or a ghastly death's head grinning at him from a darkened corner, he would hardly have been surprised. Indeed, so deep had been the effect wrought upon his imagination already that nothing, however terrifying, could have taken him completely unawares. But as it was, the utter lack of all incident upon this lonely drive wrenched at his nerves even more remorselessly than any of these things could have done, had they actually taken place.

He was no coward — in fact, more than one person would have readily described him as courageous. Yet he would have been the first to admit to a glow of relief when, on rounding the last bend, he saw ahead of him the friendly outline of the Kentish Arms. Relaxing while he bore down upon it, he fell to wondering whether Charteris would by this time have tracked down the person responsible for that unearthly laugh. But although his admiration for the inspector was great, he could not, with the best will in the world, feel anything but sceptical of his success.

As he drew to a standstill by the side door of the hostel, he saw a face quickly withdrawn from between the curtains of the lighted window beside it; and a few seconds later the door was thrown open by a radiant and smiling Judy. With friendly greetings, she directed him to the little garage adjoining the inn at the back; and following these out, he soon had his car safely locked up for the night. Returning to the house carrying his bags, his guide showed him to a neat little room, which she informed him was to be his bedsitting-room. The fact that he was to sleep on the ground floor was owing to all the other bedrooms being occupied; but she hoped he would be quite comfortable.

One look round the cheery apartment was more than sufficient to convince him that he would be, and when his eye lighted upon the tempting meal of cold ham and salad which awaited him, spread upon a spotlessly white tablecloth, his delight was completed. 'Fit for a king!' was his comment while Judy enquired what he would like to drink.

'Would it be asking you too much to make a pot of tea?'

'Of course not.'

Indeed, so strong was his influence at that moment that had he asked her to bring him a special brew from the Capital of China, it would have seemed but a trifle.

She was just opening the door when he stopped her. 'Might I suggest you bring in two cups?' he put in invitingly.

She turned as though about to refuse, but instead, on meeting his eyes, she smiled her acceptance and slipped softly from the room. Left alone, Jackson divested himself of his jacket, and sat down to partake heartily of the goodly feast before him. And for once the food tasted every bit as appetising as it looked.

While he was thus engaged, Judy returned, bringing with her a tray upon which stood two cups, besides a little milk jug and a basin of sugar. 'Is it all right?' she asked, referring to the meal, as she set this down upon the table beside him.

'Grand!' he told her. 'Have you put the kettle on?'

She nodded.

'Good. Draw a chair up then, and sit down. I want to talk to you.'

She hesitated.

'I know you're thinking I'm being a bit

101

unconventional,' he continued. 'But you can trust me; I really do want to talk to you about something.'

Upon this assurance, she obeyed, although a slight gleam of disappointment might have told a more conceited man than Conway Jackson that she would have felt far happier had he been a little less rigorously trustworthy. 'I hope you don't object to my sitting down like this?' he apologised. 'Only it's so hot. And my shirt's quite presentable, as you can see.'

'Of course I don't mind,' she assured him.

He smiled his appreciation, and tucked in with fresh relish. In between mouthfuls he talked enthusiastically about the beauty of the surrounding countryside, taking special care to mention how charming he thought the village. Interspersed with his remarks, she produced little anecdotes of her own, spiced with scraps of scandal, which were as entertaining as they were harmless.

It was not until they were sitting over their tea and cigarettes that the conversation took a more serious turn.

'What's your nearest big town here?' he enquired rather abruptly, settling himself comfortably in his chair.

'Canterbury,' she answered promptly, as though she had been asked the same question many times before.

'I suppose most of the local people do their shopping over there, don't they?' he continued in the same vein. 'Not many shops around here for them.'

'Not very many,' she admitted. 'But enough to satisfy most folk. Saturday's the time for going to Canterbury.'

'I suppose the Gleesons do all their shopping over there?'

'Not quite all,' she corrected him. 'They do come into the village every now and then. Even her ladyship's been known to do so.'

'Really?'

Having led her tactfully along the path he wished her to take, he now threw aside subterfuge, and proceeded to interrogate her after a more straightforward fashion. 'And what do you think of my aunt, Judy?'

But this question proved a little too

direct for her, so she hedged. 'It's rather difficult for me to say,' she began haltingly. 'You see, she's never been in here.'

'Naturally not,' he agreed with a smile; for the picture of his dignified aunt in a village pub was not without its more amusing aspect.

'So — so anything I know about her is — is only second-hand, as it were,' she concluded shortly.

'In other words, what you've heard from the tradespeople?'

'That's right.'

'Well, it's just what I want to hear. Go ahead! What did they say about her?'

'They — they — but really, I — '

'You're shy of telling me, because she's my aunt, aren't you?'

'Yes — er — I — '

'Don't be. I'll tell you something: by way of a hobby I'm a crime investigator. Curious pastime, isn't it? Still, it takes all sorts to make a world, as the saying has it. And at the present moment I'm all out to track down my uncle's murderer. So forget that Lady Gertrude happens to be my aunt, and just tell me all you've heard about her, will you?'

'All right, I will,' she replied, taking a gulp at her tea, as though she were about to face the Inquisition, 'though I'm afraid it doesn't sound much, when you put it into words. Mrs. Jones is the one who knows her ladyship best.'

'And who is Mrs. Jones?'

'She owns the little draper's shop on the corner. I expect you noticed it this evening?'

'As a matter of fact, I didn't. But never mind. Go on!'

'Her ladyship sometimes goes in there to buy her stockings. I suppose it's too much trouble to drag all the way over to Canterbury for them. Stockings are a big item with a woman, you know.'

'So I've been told. And what had Mrs. Jones to say about her?'

'Oh, she thought she was ever so nice. 'A nicer lady never breathed,' she used to tell me; 'and so beautiful too!''

'Used to tell you?' Jackson picked upon the words. 'Isn't my aunt still the nicest lady who ever breathed? Or has she altered?'

'I'm afraid she has,' Judy confessed with a slight return of her former embarrassment.

'How?'

'That's hard to say; but the last time she came over, she seemed quite different somehow. I passed by her in the street, and she looked as though she'd seen a ghost.'

Jackson crushed out his cigarette and leaned his elbows on the table. 'What made you think that?'

'Well, her eyes, for one thing,' she explained with difficulty. 'I've never seen anything like them. All hard they were, and stony.'

Jackson nodded thoughtfully. 'She's seen a ghost, all right,' he agreed ruminatively. 'But I'd give something to know what particular kind it was.' He turned to Judy with a smile. 'Don't pay any attention to me. I'm just soliloquising, that's all. Talking to myself. First sign of approaching lunacy, isn't it? By the way, did she have Tommy with her on the occasion you've just mentioned?'

'Yes, she did. Sweet little chap, isn't he?'

'How long ago was this? Can you remember?'

'Roughly a fortnight, I should think. No longer.'

'And how did she behave to the child?'

'Took no notice of him at all; so Mrs. Jones said.'

'Poor kid!' he murmured sympathetically. 'I'm afraid he chose a mighty bad time to get adopted. The sooner all this is cleared up the better, so far as he's concerned; then he might get a little of the affection that's due to him. But to come back to Mrs. Jones — what else did she tell you?'

'Only that her ladyship seemed all on edge, and nearly snapped her head off when she asked if she was feeling quite well.'

'Hm! Pity Mrs. Jones wasn't more of a psychologist. That's one of the main troubles with people like my aunt; if you ask them how they feel, they immediately take it as a criticism, and think you're inferring they look ill.'

'Why, that's exactly what she did! Said she felt perfectly all right, and couldn't see what Mrs. Jones wanted to ask her for. And I'm afraid that's the lot,' she finished abruptly.

'And very interesting too,' Jackson assured her. 'Were my aunt and Tommy the only people from the manor to come into the village, then?'

'Excepting one or two of the maids. Oh, and of course Mr. Rogers.'

'The butler? What do you think of him?'

'I haven't seen enough of him to say properly. But Dad doesn't like him much.'

'I expect your father sizes up the customers pretty quickly, doesn't he?'

'Yes, he does.'

'Well in the case of Mr. Rogers, I'm inclined to agree with him. But don't any of the guests from the manor look in for a drink now and then?'

Judy shook her head. 'There haven't been any guests for a long time. People down in the Hollow say the Gleesons haven't enough money to entertain much.'

'I should think that's perfectly true.'

'I believe Mr. Burke, the gentleman who writes books, has been in; but that was when Dad was behind the bar.'

'Writes books, does he?' Jackson cried in surprise. 'I never knew that!'

'Didn't you?' She looked at him in genuine surprise, such as one might bestow upon an illiterate who had never heard of Shakespeare or Dickens. 'Why, he writes those adventure stories in *The Purple Mag*. I remember now it was he who told Dad about the famous pianist they've got staying up there.'

'Fritz Hoffman, you mean?'

'That's the name! Never heard of him myself. But he's going to play for us at the charity concert the night after tomorrow.'

'Great Scott! Fritz Hoffman is?'

'Yes. Young Master Tommy told him about it, it seems. He's going to recite — and he offered his services right away, without even waiting to be asked.'

So, Fritz Hoffman, the world famous pianist, was going to play at the village hall in Hamlin Hollow! There was a real act of charity, thought Jackson admiringly.

'Perhaps you'd like to come too?' Judy went on, heedless of the effect her words had produced upon the listener. 'It's only next door, and the tickets — ' She stopped dead in the middle of the sentence, interrupted by a furtive rapping from the outside door. 'Now who on earth can that be?' she exclaimed in a hushed voice as Jackson darted a swift glance in the direction from whence the sound had come.

'I don't know,' he answered, rising to his feet. 'But wait here while I find out.' Noiselessly he left the room and crept out into the little hall beyond.

It was by this time nearing midnight, a most unpropitious hour for visitors. A slight feeling of apprehension took hold of him as he approached the door. Suddenly he realised he was completely unarmed. He possessed a fairly serviceable pair of fists, it was true; but should this nocturnal visitor carry a gun by any chance, these would prove of little use.

For a second he stood in the darkness, undecided; then he stretched one hand cautiously forward. Luckily the door was unlocked, and with a swift movement he turned the handle and threw it open, taking good care to step back into the shadows as he did so.

Outlined against the dimness without was the figure of a man.

'Yes? What do you want?' Jackson demanded tentatively, careful not to move into the other's line of sight.

There was a slight pause; then: 'Mr. Jackson?' enquired a voice out of the darkness.

'Yes. Why, it's you!'

With this startled exclamation, Jackson stepped forward. 'Come in,' he invited curiously.

And without another word, Frederick Gleeson stepped over the threshold!

8

'Unfinished Symphony'

As Conway Jackson's Alvis disappeared round the bend of the drive, Inspector Charteris looked about him. Everything seemed quiet as the proverbial graveyard. And had he not a few minutes ago been in the company of somebody who could bear witness to what he had heard, he might have felt inclined to disbelieve the evidence of his own senses.

The house stood out before him in bold relief against the almost tropical splendour of the sky. Had that discordant laugh come from the building or the garden? Intently he scanned the latter; the trees and bushes blended oddly with the gloom, seeming to make one composite pattern without beginning or end.

No use searching among those, he told himself. Better confine his attentions to the house; there at least he had a reasonable chance of success. For as far as he knew, all the inmates, with the exception of Miss Harcourt, the child, and Lady Gertrude, who was still presumably in her boudoir, were in the music-room.

That ghoulish chuckle could not have come from either a child or a woman; its sex, so far as it had any, being definitely masculine. Thus, by the simple process of elimination, the person responsible must be in the last named place. Unless, of course, it should turn out to be one of the servants. For a moment he paused to consider this possibility; then made up his mind to try the music-room first.

With this end in view, he made his way down the passage towards the rear of the house. Very unobtrusively, he let himself into the music-room. As he did so, he was greeted by a burst of conversation. The windows were still open, and the room dimly lit by the one lamp which stood beside the piano; cigarettes glowed redly in the darkness while the dim figure of the butler flitted silently from one to the other of them, with a tray of drinks.

Eyeing him along with the four other occupants of the room, Charteris fell to conjecturing if it were possible for one of them to have slipped round to the front and returned again before his own entrance. Having decided it was, he set about satisfying himself upon this point right away.

The first person to be questioned was Rogers. This came about quite naturally as he approached the inspector with the offer of refreshment.

'Have you been out in the garden recently?' Charteris asked him in a monotone, waving aside the drinks.

'No, sir. I've been down in the kitchen for the past half hour,' the man answered in astonishment.

'Any of the other servants been out? Make up your mind before you answer now!'

'No, sir. They're all downstairs, playing cards.'

'You're sure they're all there?'

'Yes, sir. Quite sure, sir.'

'Very well. That'll do!'

Only too glad to get away, Rogers was

114

out of the room like a streak of lightning.

As Charteris turned his gaze upon the others, Gleeson and Fritz Hoffman, who had been engaged in deep conversation in one of the far corners, advanced to meet him.

'Not drinking, Inspector?' queried the former. 'How's that?'

'Keeping my head clear for my job,' Charteris explained briefly.

'And how are things progressing?' chimed in the melodious tones of Fritz Hoffman.

'Not very well, I'm afraid. Have either of you two gentlemen been out in the garden during the last few minutes?'

'I have,' Gleeson owned up promptly. 'Only just come in.'

'Did you hear anything — unusual?'

'I don't know what you mean by 'unusual', Inspector. But I heard nothing at all. Why do you ask?'

'And you, Mr. Hoffman?' Charteris proceeded, ignoring the question. 'Have you been out lately?'

The musician shook his head with a smile. 'I've had enough fresh air for one day,' he declared with a little twinkle in his eyes. 'So I've not moved from this room all evening.'

'I can bear witness to that,' declared Gleeson.

'Oh no, you can't! He might quite easily have slipped out while you were in the garden.'

'That's true, Inspector,' Hoffman agreed affably. 'So I could, if I had wanted to. But you see, I didn't.'

'Maybe the other two will be able to corroborate that statement?'

Hoffman indicated Joan and Pat, seated together at the opposite end of the room, with a graceful gesture of the hand. 'I don't think they're in a fit state to corroborate anything at the moment. Look at them! They haven't noticed that you've entered the room yet; why should they have observed me then, if I'd left it? No, Inspector — I'm sorry, but I'm afraid you'll have to be satisfied with my bare word.'

Seeing the truth of this, the inspector replied with a characteristic grunt, which brought a dark flush of anger to the great musician's cheek. 'Is it so very difficult to believe, then?' Hoffman demanded heatedly. 'I'm not in the habit of lying, Inspector Charteris!'

'I'm sure you're not,' the inspector retorted in a more conciliatory vein. 'I never imagined for a moment that you were.'

'Thank you!'

Hoffman gave Charteris a stiff bow, as the latter made his way across the floor towards the lovers. With their faces very close together, they continued in their animated discourse until he was within a few paces of them. Then, becoming suddenly conscious of his presence, they looked up, for all the world like a couple of startled and embarrassed children. Had he been feeling in a kinder frame of mind, he would have regarded them as something rather charming — which, in fact, they were; but as it was, he saw nothing beyond two rather unsatisfactory witnesses.

'I don't suppose either of you has been in the garden lately?' he remarked; and they shook their heads innocently. 'But have you noticed anybody else going out there?' he persisted.

'I haven't,' replied Joan artlessly.

Looking full into her soft appealing eyes, he sought to gauge whether or not she was lying; but they stared back at him, filled with an untroubled serenity that defied all probing. Baffled, he shifted his gaze to her companion. 'Have you?'

The young man met his look unfalteringly. 'I'm afraid not,' he answered. 'Why, should I have done?'

Before Charteris had time to frame a reply to this rather disconcerting question, he was prevented by a query from Frederick Gleeson, who, unknown to him, was standing at his side.

'Might we enquire what it was that took place in the garden, Inspector, since you seem to attach so much importance to it?' he asked suavely, as Charteris turned away from Joan to face him.

'Something rather unpleasant,' he said, endeavouring to take in the entire room, including the dark corner which concealed Fritz Hoffman. 'It happened while I was seeing Mr. Jackson into his car — '

'Seeing Cousin Jaggers into his car?' Joan demanded, suddenly coming to life and sitting bolt upright. 'Where's he gone to?'

'The Kentish Arms, Miss Gleeson; to spend the night there.'

'But why? Hasn't he seen Lady Gertrude?'

'Yes, he's seen her,' he said in a voice grown considerably kinder, 'but she told him — '

'That the house was full?'

'Yes.'

'What a lie! What a damned, wicked lie!' the woman burst out hotly.

'Joan! Dearest!' Pat took her by the arm, but she shook him off impatiently.

'She didn't want him to stay because she was afraid of him! She's heard how clever he is from Father, and she's terrified he might find his murderer!'

'Why should she be afraid of that, Miss Gleeson?' Charteris cut in.

'Because she knows who killed him, that's why!'

'Joan! Whatever are you saying?' It was Fritz Hoffman who addressed her now, and he sounded horrified.

'And why shouldn't he know the truth? That's what he's here for, isn't it?' she went on hotly. 'She's been behaving queerly for ages. And do you know why?' she addressed them all. 'Because she knew all the time that it was going to happen, of course!'

'Stop it, Joan!' Pat cried. 'Just because your stepmother's been a little offhand with everybody for the past few weeks, you're accusing her of being an accessory to murder! Do you realise what you're saying? As though she would hurt your father, when she loved him as much as you did!'

Suddenly, without any warning, Joan burst into a flood of tears, burying her face against his shoulder. By common consent, the three other men moved away to a more secluded part of the room, leaving the youngest of their party to cope with an emergency that he had proved himself more capable of handling than any of them.

'Of course, she's just very upset, Inspector,' Hoffman explained softly as they turned their backs upon the young couple by the window. 'She doesn't mean it. She's very fond of her stepmother, really.'

'I'm sure she is,' the inspector replied absent-mindedly. To himself, however, he was thinking how well Joan's little outburst fitted in with what he and Jackson already suspected of Lady Gertrude; and he resolved to tell that young man all she had said at the very first opportunity.

'You were about to tell us what happened in the garden, were you not?' Hoffman continued in a tactful attempt to draw his attention from the scene of a few moments ago.

'Yes. As I was seeing Mr. Jackson into his car,' Charteris picked up the narrative from where he'd left off, 'we heard a laugh — not an ordinary laugh, mind you, but a sound such as could have been made only by somebody possessed of an utterly inhuman malignity!'

'Where did this come from?' Gleeson enquired intently; so intently that the inspector looked at him.

'We're not sure,' he said, watching the other's face closely, 'but we think it was from the house.'

With great difficulty, Gleeson struggled with something very like a smile of triumph.

'You seem very interested, Mr. Gleeson,' the inspector observed.

'Nonsense, Inspector,' the other replied with an unconvincing show of carelessness. 'I'm intrigued, that's all. And who wouldn't be, by such a macabre story?'

'If you're doubting the truth of what I've just told you, you're making the greatest mistake of your life,' the inspector retaliated quietly. 'I don't wish to scare anybody, but there's some evil influence still at work in this house. If any of you know anything you've not yet divulged, now's the time to get it off your chests. And remember, murderers seldom stop at one crime: the death of Sir James may only be the beginning. So take my advice, and tread warily!'

'Really, Inspector, it sounds as though you were threatening us.'

A light touch on Charteris's elbow

brought him round to Joan, with her eyes dried. 'I hope you won't take what I said about Lady Gertrude too seriously, Inspector,' she said. 'I didn't mean it. She loved Daddy, I know. I'm quite myself again now.'

'Certainly, Miss Gleeson, if you wish it,' Charteris lied convincingly.

With a sigh of relief and a little smile of gratitude, she returned to Pat by the window.

'There! What did I say?' Hoffman declared with an expansive gesture. 'She was just upset.'

The inspector nodded. But had the other occupants of the room known what was going on inside his brain, they would have realised that a police officer, in common with an elephant, never forgets!

'A little music might help proceedings at this juncture, don't you think?' the musician went on, having darted a mischievous glance at the two in the corner; and in answer to an absent-minded nod from the inspector, he seated himself at the piano.

Surely never in the whole course of his

career could he have played to a less enthusiastic audience! The lovers, it's true, favoured him with their almost undivided attention; but Gleeson curtly excused himself, and retired to bed; while the inspector, although he sank down quietly enough into the nearest armchair, showed clearly by his every expression that he was feeling distinctly uncomfortable, lest the great pianist intended to inflict upon him a Bach prelude or one of the numerous other compositions that even the BBC was powerless to make acceptable to his decidedly lowbrow tastes.

Sensing this lack of concord among his audience, Hoffman decided upon a compromise, and chose the charming and melodious works of Franz Schubert. These suited all tastes, and as he slipped gracefully from one passage to another, the listeners forgot their own personal problems and soon joined in the mood with him.

Gradually he had drifted into the *Unfinished Symphony*. By this time, his audience was held spellbound. Genius had triumphed with all of them; and even the unsusceptible inspector was — for perhaps the first and only time in his life — carried completely away, far beyond the bounds of sordid reality. Not a sound, bar the cascade of liquid notes, broke the stillness of the softly lit room.

Then Joan gave a startled cry: 'Look — across the lawn!'

Suddenly, everything was plunged into pandemonium. The music stopped abruptly, and all four of them rushed to the window. They saw what she was referring to at once: the figure of a man running furtively across the lawn, suitcase in hand, towards the belt of trees, from where it was obvious he intended to make for the road that led to the village!

Without hesitating, the burly inspector shot out into the garden, and across the path onto the lawn. Everything had happened so speedily that he'd found no time to observe what the others were doing, but he soon became aware that he was not alone in his pursuit. Pat Burke, running with all the ease and precision of the trained athlete, overtook and passed him. As this happened, their quarry, after a hurried glance round at his pursuers, disappeared through the trees. The very next second, there was the barking of a dog.

Putting on a spurt, Pat raced forwards, and was soon through the belt of trees. The barking had by this time died down to a menacing growl; and when Inspector Charteris, panting and dripping with sweat, finally emerged upon the scene, most of the fun was over. The quarry lay stretched out upon the ground, vainly striving to beat off the huge collie that had succeeded in burying its teeth in one of his trouser legs, while Pat was doing all in his power to pull the great brute off from his back.

When all his efforts proved useless, a cry of 'Bob' from the cottage succeeded; and old Ferguson, with a threadbare coat thrown heedlessly over his night attire, came hobbling towards them. At the same time, Joan and Hoffman came running up, the party thus forming themselves into a semicircle around the prostrate man.

Scared but unhurt, Rogers rose to his feet, casting a frightened glance at the dog, which stood beside its master, its teeth bared in preparation for renewing the attack at any minute.

'I only wanted to get away, Inspector,' he whined. 'I haven't done anything — honest, I haven't!'

'Sure?' queried the inspector unsympathetically, darting a glance to where lay his suitcase, which had burst open in the fray. 'Since when have you taken to wearing diamond bracelets, eh, Rogers?'

'My diamonds!' cried Joan, throwing the lid back even further.

'And my pearl studs!' echoed Hoffman.

'We'll give you another pair of bracelets for these, my lad,' the inspector snapped authoritatively. 'They may not be quite so elegant, but you'll find them more to your style.'

And with Joan carrying the suitcase, and Hoffman going on ahead, he and Pat marched the erring butler back to the house.

9

The Black Shape Again!

Silently, Jackson closed the door behind his visitor and preceded him into the lighted room. At their entrance, Judy rose to her feet.

'It's all right, my dear,' he assured her. 'This is Mr. Gleeson — my uncle's brother, from the manor. Mr. Gleeson, this is the one and only Judy.'

Rather self-consciously, the two people thus unexpectedly brought together shook hands. And in the pause that followed, Judy edged towards the door.

'If you don't mind, Mr. Jackson, I think I'll be getting along to bed now. You'll lock up after Mr. Gleeson, won't you?'

'I will.'

'Oh — and what time d'you want to be called in the morning?'

'Not a second before ten,' he ordered sternly. 'With breakfast.'

'In bed?'

'No, not quite so decadent as all that; very nearly, though! Just bring in a nice breakfast, please, put it on the table, and shake me half a dozen times. And by the way, don't be too gentle or I shall only go off to sleep again.'

'Very well; I'll see to that myself. Good night. Good night, Mr. Gleeson.' And amid murmured good nights from the two men, she withdrew.

Jackson motioned Gleeson to a chair. 'Afraid I can't offer you anything,' he apologised, seating himself opposite him.

'That's all right. Mind if I smoke?'

'Not at all.'

Producing a pipe, he filled and lit it. He seemed to be finding some difficulty in beginning what he had come to say; this did not worry Jackson, however, for it gave him a fresh opportunity of observing the man at close quarters. The impression he drew was not very complimentary. The large florid face, with its bleary eyes and thick sensual lips, were scarcely features calculated to endear him to anybody. His hoarse voice and ponderous way of speaking were also against him. No, try as he might, Jackson could find nothing to recommend him; the man seemed thoroughly unpleasant from every point of view.

His pipe now drawing to his satisfaction, Gleeson leaned back in his chair, emitting a cloud of somewhat foul-smelling smoke, which he watched in silent meditation as it ascended in spirals towards the ceiling. Then, just as Jackson was beginning to experience the first pangs of impatience, he spoke: 'I gather, Mr. Jackson, you're figuring on taking part in the investigation into my brother James's death? Am I right?'

'You are.' The man had obviously come to tell him something important, so it seemed diplomatic to put him at his ease as far as possible. 'But what gave you the idea?' he queried, more eager to extract information than to give it.

'Your acquaintanceship with Inspector Charteris, for one thing. You've been holding conferences together, on and off, ever since you came to the house. Also, I'd heard of you from my brother. You and he were great friends at one time, weren't you?'

'We were. And if I'd had my way, we should have remained so until his death.'

'Your father, of course, was the stumbling block to that. In some ways he was right, though, you know. Poor old James was always rather the failure of the family . . . '

For several minutes, he rambled on in a recital of his brother's misdeeds — a dissertation calculated to put his hearer against him, if anything was! — until Jackson decided it was high time he broke in upon it and forced from him the reason for his call.

'Surely you've not come all this way just to tell me of Uncle James's misdeeds, when you could have done so in far greater comfort at the manor, Uncle Frederick?'

'Uncle Frederick', thus addressed, eyed his nephew suspiciously — not at all sure whether he was being rude. 'You're right. I came for something quite different.'

He indulged in a second pause, which lasted until Jackson felt that if there was another minute of it, he would scream. Gleeson's next remark, however, made up amply for the delay.

'I came to tell you that I've seen my brother's murderer.'

Jackson sat up with a start. 'You've seen him?' he cried.

'Him — her — it, whatever you choose to call it.'

'Have you told the inspector this?'

'No.'

'Good heavens, man! Whyever not?'

'Because I was requested not to.'

'By whom?'

'Can I have your word that you won't repeat it if I tell you?'

'I'll promise to use my discretion.'

'That's hardly the same, is it?'

Maybe it was the slight movement on Gleeson's part that gave him the impression, but for one agonising moment he felt the man was going to leave — and, still worse, take his secret with him. 'Think what you're up against!' he burst out vehemently. 'If you don't tell either me or the inspector, you'll be putting yourself in the position of an accessory.'

'I know; that's why I've come to you tonight,' the other replied, unmoved by the younger man's passion.

'Because I'm a member of the family?'

'That was my primary reason, yes.'

'Thank the Lord it's done me some good at last!' Jackson declared with a short laugh. 'It didn't help much with Aunt Gertrude.'

Gleeson raised a pair of dull eyes to his. 'Will you tell me something?'

'If I can.'

'How long were you standing outside Gertrude's boudoir before I came out?'

'Just long enough to hear her warn you to go away, that's all.'

'Thank you.'

'Oh, you needn't feel you're under any obligation to confide in me because of that,' Jackson went on, conscious that he was losing ground badly. 'But your behaviour in coming here tonight has definitely shown that you know something, and it leaves me no choice but to mention as much to Inspector Charteris.'

'Unless I give you my reason; then you'll use your discretion?'

'I've already told you so.'

'In that case, you leave me with no alternative. But remember, I'm telling you this as a member of the family; and I hope you'll think very carefully before you divulge it to anybody outside our immediate circle. It happened like this.

'On the night that James met his death, I retired to bed at eleven o'clock, along with all the others. Unfortunately, I'm a very bad sleeper; in fact, some nights it takes two or three hours before I succeed in dozing off, and even then it's quite often fitful and unsatisfactory. On the night in question, my head had no sooner touched the pillow than I was wide awake.

'Downstairs I had felt ready for sleep, but I knew, as I twisted and turned in the stifling darkness of that broiling night, I was in for one of my bad spells. I'm telling you this because it accounts for the fact that I was still quite conscious when the clock in Hamlin Hollow struck midnight, and it also explains why I was roused upon the instant by my brother's scream.

'As you've doubtless noticed, Gleeson Manor is a double-fronted house, and my bedroom is at the back, over the music-room; whilst the bedroom across the hall is over the study. Well, as soon as I heard the scream, I sprang out of bed and ran barefooted to the window. That it had come from below, I was certain; but whether it had originated in the house or the garden, it was no easy matter to decide. Throwing back the curtains, I put my head out of the open window.

'At first I saw nothing but the peacefulness of a summer's night; but then, just as I was about to withdraw into the room again, I noticed something very different! Through the French windows leading out of the study crept a black shape. There was something revolting in the stealth with which it slithered into the bright moonlight of the garden. Running along, so close to the ground that for one moment I was almost convinced it was an animal, it swarmed up the drainpipe and climbed through the window into the room on the opposite side of the passage to mine!'

'Good God!' Jackson exclaimed, unable to control his excitement any longer. 'But whose bedroom is that?'

'Miss Harcourt's,' came the soft reply.

So I was right when I told Charteris she knew something, Jackson thought. *And the tale about the black shape 'running close to the ground' — the very words the gardener used! There must be something in that, too!* In the midst of all these speculations, he became aware that his visitor was still talking.

'And now I'm reaching the part I want you to keep a secret, for it concerns your Aunt Gertrude.'

Jackson became all attention.

'Pushing my feet into my slippers, and throwing a dressing gown around myself, I ran out into the passage. I was about to burst into Miss Harcourt's room, hoping to surprise her, when I was prevented. Gertrude, who'd just come out of her room, cried to me to stop. Catching hold of my arm, she began to pull me away. I tried to explain to her, but she refused to listen; and before I knew what had happened, she'd led me downstairs, and we were standing with the others in the study.'

'But did you let it rest there?' Jackson demanded.

'No, I didn't,' Gleeson replied with an air of pride. 'I made an effort to slip out of the room, seeing that Miss Harcourt wasn't there; but again Gertrude forestalled me. Taking my arm, she accompanied me out into the hall, where, to my astonishment, we encountered Miss Harcourt herself, coming down the stairs! She said she'd just succeeded in getting Tommy off to sleep again, and asked us what had happened. I told her, and — '

'Did she seem surprised?'

'Yes, but — I don't know whether I'm right to say this — I felt it was all rather overdone.'

'Acting, in fact?'

'Yes. Then the three of us went into the music-room.'

'How about the others in the study? Didn't they wonder what'd become of you?'

'I don't think so. You see, they were all too upset to notice anything; and even if they did, I don't expect they'd attach much importance to it.'

'Go on.'

'Well, we argued awhile; and then I lost control of myself and accused them of harbouring a murderer.'

'How did they react to that?'

'At first they laughed. And to prove I'd been having 'delusions', as they termed them, they took me up to Miss Harcourt's room to show me nobody was there. Then, when this failed to convince me, Gertrude sent Miss Harcourt away, and implored me not to tell the police.'

'But by doing that, she must have admitted its authenticity?'

'No, she didn't. She talked a great deal about it throwing unnecessary suspicion on Miss Harcourt, and how fond she was of her — but it wasn't any of that which made me hold my tongue: it was her face! I haven't been a friend of Gertrude's at any time — or she of mine, for that matter; but I've never seen anybody going through such hell as she was in at that moment!'

'What sort of hell d'you mean?'

'I don't know — terror, agony; it's hard to explain in words.'

'Not sorrow?'

'Strange to say, no.'

There it was again! Terror and agony, but not sorrow. What did it mean? 'So you promised her not to tell?'

'Yes. It was much against my will, but I did. Then we returned to the study, where we waited until the police appeared.'

'I see. And in Aunt Gertrude's boudoir this evening, I presume you were asking for permission to retract your promise?'

'Without success.'

'Did she still persist in denying the truth of what you said you'd seen?'

'Yes; although by the look in her eyes, it was plain to see she knew it was true, as I did.'

'And how did she come to threaten you?'

'Quite suddenly. I frightened her by saying I should break the promise, whether she gave me leave or no. At this, she implored me to go. Then, when I refused, she threatened me.'

'I see. Hardly very consistent, was she?'

Now he could understand why she had been so anxious to know how much he'd overheard. Seen in this light, there could be no possible doubt that she knew the identity of her husband's murderer, and was prepared to shield him at all costs! But why?

A slight pause had followed Gleeson's last answer and Jackson's comment upon it, which was now broken by the former rising to his feet. 'And that's the whole story, for what it's worth!' he declared with finality as he pocketed his pipe, long since burnt out. 'If you want to ask me any further questions, you can see me up at the manor in the morning.'

'There's one I'd like to ask you right now,' Jackson replied softly.

'Well? Let's have it.'

'Have you any suspicion of your own as to the identity of that black shape you saw?'

Gleeson looked at him for a few moments before replying. Then: 'I'd rather not say at the moment.'

Jackson shrugged his shoulders. 'Very well. Have you a car?' he enquired politely as they walked towards the door.

'Yes. But I left it in town.'

'Do you mean to say you walked?'

'I did. And don't I know it. Haven't taken so much exercise for years. Rather lucky I did, though, for had I been driving I should probably have been spotted by Inspector Kennedy; I passed him in his car on the way, but he didn't notice me.'

'He must have been going up to fetch Charteris. Sure you wouldn't rather stay here? I can fix you up on a couch or something.'

'No thanks; I'd rather get back.'

'Shall I walk part of the way with you?'

'Heavens, no! It's a lovely night; I shall enjoy it.'

'Just as you like. By the way, how did you know I was staying here?'

'Inspector Charteris told us. You should have heard what Joan had to say about it — but that's another story, and I want to get to bed!'

'Did the inspector tell you about what we heard in the garden, by any chance?'

'The laugh, you mean? Yes, he did. It was that, on top of everything else, that finally decided me to come and tell you all I knew.'

'Well, many thanks for coming. You've given me a lot to think about.'

Gleeson chuckled. 'Given myself a pretty good bit to think about too! You'll try not to put Gertrude against me over all this, though, won't you?'

'I'll do my best, I promise you.'

'Thanks.' Buttoning up his jacket, the man stepped out into the lane.

'Hope you enjoy your walk,' Jackson whispered cheerily.

'I expect I shall; this sort of thing's new to me. See you tomorrow!'

'Good night!'

Thoughtfully, Jackson bolted the door and returned to the sitting-room. His Uncle Frederick certainly *had* given him something to think about! And it was nearly dawn before he put out the lamp and rolled wearily into bed.

★   ★   ★

Humming a music-hall ditty in a rather cracked and discordant voice, Frederick

Gleeson swung along the narrow road leading to the manor. He couldn't remember when he'd felt in such good spirits! Ever since his brother's death, he'd been miserable as hell; not because he'd lost a brother, but because in holding his peace concerning what he'd seen in the garden, he was falling foul of the police. There was something about that he didn't quite care for. Honesty was never one of his outstanding qualities, but keeping barely within the limits of the law was. To him, the police were people to steer clear of; and although in the course of his shady business career he had done several dirty tricks, he'd never been responsible for anything that could be definitely thought of as illegal: an accomplishment of which he was inordinately proud.

Well, now he'd told them, at any rate — or rather, told Jaggers, which amounted to the same thing; and maybe they'd soon reach the same conclusion regarding the identity of the murderer as he had.

Rounding the last bend, he found himself within sight of the manor, and began fishing around in this trouser pocket for the key. That key was about to come in rather useful, he meditated; it had been given to him in the first place in order to stop him from waking the inmates when returning from what he tersely described as a 'blind', over at Canterbury.

As his hand closed over the familiar object, he became conscious of a sudden feeling of alarm. He was not a man of intuition; and yet upon this occasion, he could feel a distinct chill somewhere in the region of his spine.

Increasing his pace, he resolutely sought to drown his fears in a renewal of the ditty; but somehow the words refused to come, for the reason that his throat had become curiously dry. Not a sound, save the crunching of his own boots on the dusty road, disturbed the countryside for miles around. He could see it stretched out before him like a vast panorama. Then things slowly began to grow dimmer.

Looking up, he saw this was due to the moon passing behind a cloud. It was only a fleecy summer cloud, but nevertheless, the momentary dimness broke down his powers of control; and all at once he found himself running as fast as his legs could carry him, with the clammy sweat streaming at every pore.

He had just passed by the little gate leading into the grounds when he came upon the unseen cause of his sudden apprehensions. Out of the bushes at the side of the road, something sprang upon him!

It was at the moment when the moon was at its faintest. The impact sent him reeling backwards, full length on to the road; and as he opened his mouth to cry out, he saw two blazing eyes glaring down at him.

The vampire man!

Two soft, seductive hands curled themselves around his throat; and as they turned into remorseless tentacles, a horribly quiet and insane chuckle seared itself into his consciousness.

He longed to cry out, but he couldn't; to struggle, but all strength seemed to have left his body! A deathly inertia began to steal over him . . . eyes, huge luminous eyes; and hands, crushing, relentless hands; sinking . . . sinking . . . sinking . . .

The moon soon passed from behind the cloud, and once again the countryside was bathed in its gentle radiance. But by this time, such things held no further significance for the still form that had once been Frederick Gleeson!

10

In the Shadow of Death

Despite several vigorous shakings administered by Judy, it was considerably nearer half-past ten than it was to ten when Jackson finally rolled out of bed and, wrapping his dressing-gown negligently around him, staggered in a sort of daze to the breakfast table.

The good old conventional meal of eggs and bacon followed by toast and marmalade, with a really vast cup of tea to wash it all down, did much to revive him. But he was barely halfway through this delicious repast when Charteris arrived. Ordering another cup, Jackson asked him to be seated, and pushed his cigarette case across to him.

The inspector was obviously worried, and it was equally obvious that he was determined not to speak of what was on his mind until they were alone; so Jackson

147

had to possess himself of patience until Judy had brought his cup and departed again.

'Well, now perhaps you'll tell me what's worrying you?' he suggested, handing the inspector a steaming cup of tea. 'You look as though you'd been to twenty inquests instead of one — and while we're on the subject of inquests, what was the verdict?'

'What we expected: 'murder against person or persons unknown'. But it's not the verdict that's worrying me.'

'What is it, then?'

'There's been another murder, Jaggers.'

Jackson gave a long whistle. 'Whew! Who is it, this time?'

'Sir James's brother, Frederick. Inspector Kennedy found his body at the side of the road when he drove up to the manor this morning to fetch some notes I'd left behind. How he happened to be there, nobody knows; he said he was going to bed the last time I saw him.'

'I can clear that up,' Jackson explained quietly. 'He'd been to see me.'

'Here, do you mean?' the inspector demanded in surprise.

'Yes. He'd heard you say I was staying at the Kentish Arms, so he walked all the way down to see me. He left here at about two o'clock, with the intention of walking back. How he proposed to let himself in, I don't know. You must have been at Kennedy's place by then, or you'd have passed him on the road. Where did you say he was found?'

'At the side of the road — just past the little gate leading to the manor grounds. But what on earth did he mean by slipping down here after he'd said he was going to bed?'

'He came to tell me the same story as the gardener. He claims to have looked out of his window and seen that black shape too.'

'Great Scott! Why didn't he tell me when I questioned him?'

'Because my aunt had persuaded him not to.'

'Oh, that was kind of her! But what made him look out of the window in the first place?'

'He heard the scream and wasn't sure whether it had come from the house or the grounds. His bedroom's over the music-room; and he claimed he saw the black shape come out of the study and climb the drainpipe into Miss Harcourt's room, which is across the passage from his.'

'Well, that looks as though it might lead somewhere. Rather fits in with your theory about her being in some way involved in it, doesn't it? Did he try to question her, d'you know?'

'Yes. He tried to force an entrance into her room also, but on both occasions my aunt prevented him.'

'Hm. She seems to be in it as deeply as anyone.'

'I'm afraid she is. But I've very little hope of getting anything out of her. I suppose you've broken the news of Uncle Frederick's death to her?'

Charteris shook his head and flushed uncomfortably. 'I'm — er — afraid not,' he stammered. 'I've told all the others, but — you see, we — er — I was hoping you'd do that, seeing you're her nephew.'

Jackson looked up in surprise. 'If it's a member of the family you're after, what's wrong with Joan?' he asked.

'Nothing. Only — well, to be frank, I thought, what with the shock and everything, if you handled it carefully, you — er — '

'Might be able to get something out of her?' Jackson suggested, helping him out.

'Exactly. I know it's taking advantage of an unfortunate situation, Jaggers,' Charteris sought to excuse himself, 'but one doesn't like to neglect any opportunity.'

'I understand. It's the old case of being a police officer first, and a human being second. That's one of the reasons why I never joined the force. Here, have another cup of tea.'

'But you'll do it, Jaggers, won't you?' the other enquired anxiously as he handed over his cup.

'Yes, I'll do it. But you must give me a little while to decide what I'm going to say to her. It's liable to be a pretty ticklish situation.'

'Oh, that's all right. We'll give you time to think it over,' the inspector promised as he received his replenished cup. 'As a matter of fact, I was about to suggest a little trip to Canterbury before we return to the manor.'

'Why on earth Canterbury?'

'For two reasons: one, because Gleeson's body is there — they hadn't room for it here — and two, because that's where Rogers has been taken.'

'Rogers? The butler?'

'Yes. Oh, I forgot to tell you about that, didn't I?'

Briefly he outlined to Jackson what had transpired following Joan's cry about somebody running across the lawn, concluding: 'Nothing could shake him in his assertion that he was only trying to run away, and had no connection with the murder. He's done time on several occasions for petty thefts and the like, so apparently the mere sight of a police officer was sufficient to send him scampering. According to him, he'd been trying to run straight, and was terrified when the murder took place, lest his former record might be held against him. That was his reason for attempting a moonlight flit instead of giving in his notice in the more conventional way.'

'But how did he account for the presence of the jewellery in his case?'

'That, he admits, was a lapse. He had evidently made up his mind to depart early in the day, and had all his things packed in readiness. When the hour arrived, however, his past habits came up to face him, and he felt compelled to take away a few souvenirs. It says much for his taste that he chose the most valuable 'souvenirs' he could find.'

Jackson laughed. 'Sounds as though the man might have become a psychologist, had he not taken the wrong turning.'

Charteris grunted. 'I fail to see much psychologist about it,' he growled. 'I'm hoping a night in the jug will have made him see things more clearly. I've got to charge him before the magistrate at Canterbury this morning anyway, so it might be worthwhile questioning him, don't you think?'

'Certainly. I'd like to have a look at that body too. If you'll go over and chat to Inspector Kennedy, I'll guarantee to have the car outside the station in fifteen minutes.'

And he was as good as his word, or rather better, for it actually lacked one minute to the fifteen when his long streamlined car drew to a standstill outside the compact stone building.

Having been on the lookout, Charteris and Kennedy immediately joined him.

'I never asked if you'd care to see Sir James's body,' the former said. 'It's in the little temporary mortuary we've rigged up at the back here. Would you like to?'

'No, thanks,' Jackson declined with a shake of the head. 'I'm not out to see more bodies than I have to, and poor Uncle James's is not likely to tell us much at this stage. I suppose the funeral will be allowed to take place now?'

Charteris nodded as he seated himself beside the wheel. 'I've told Miss Gleeson this morning. She's making all the arrangements.'

Jackson turned to Inspector Kennedy, who seemed to be standing rather aimlessly at the side of the car. 'Are you coming along too, Inspector?' he enquired with a polite smile.

'That was the idea, Mr. Jackson,' the

pleasant-looking official confessed. 'I'm going to sit on your tail, so to speak. That's my car behind you.' He pointed to a rather dilapidated Ford several paces in the rear of the Alvis, looking somewhat like a tramp in the train of a king.

'If you don't mind squeezing in, I'd be delighted to take you along with us,' Jackson offered.

'Thank you very much, Mr. Jackson. That would certainly be simpler, wouldn't it?'

So it was arranged; and a few minutes later, the three of them started out on their roundabout way to Canterbury — roundabout because they'd decided not to pass Gleeson Manor; the reason for this being that since the place appeared to be sheltering a murderer, it seemed advisable to keep their movements as much to themselves as possible.

The day was perfect, hardly a cloud in sight and — for the first time that week — a gentle breeze to fan their cheeks. Under ordinary circumstances, Jackson would have enjoyed the drive immensely; but on this particular occasion, he was far too worried to appreciate it.

Carefully he went back over his conversation with the man whose cold body now awaited them in the mortuary at Canterbury. The reason for his death seemed an obvious one. In common with Lady Gertrude, he evidently knew the identity of the murderer, although he had refused to divulge it. This made him a menace, especially as he had already taken to paying his nephew visits in the middle of the night for the purpose of exchanging confidences. Could it be that Sir James had unmasked the criminal also? That would certainly provide a motive for his death, anyway.

Transferring his thoughts to more pressing things, he turned to Charteris. 'I believe Joan made a bit of a scene on my account last night?'

'She most certainly did,' agreed the inspector. 'Why . . . '

By the time he'd finished his detailed recital of all Joan had said in her little outburst, they were passing through the West Gate into the City of Canterbury. Despite all their troubles of the moment, this beautiful old-world spot, with its picturesque winding streets over which the tall cathedral spires brooded like some protecting angel, exerted the same influence of peace and well-being over them as it had always done. Nothing ever seemed to wake it out of its blissful slumber. True, it altered in some respects — new buildings sprang up here and there, while others were demolished in order to make way for them — but fundamentally the atmosphere remained unchanged; thoughtful and soothing to the jagged nerves.

It was not long before they reached the police station, and in a very few minutes they were looking down upon the unsightly object stretched out upon a marble slab, which comprised all the mortal remains of Frederick Gleeson. In death, the face that in life had been far from prepossessing was unimaginably ghastly. The neck showed as one purple bruise.

'No amateur did that,' Jackson commented, pointing to it. 'It's the work of a professional strangler.'

'But this is what I can't understand,' said Charteris, drawing back the sheet that covered the body, thereby revealing the soiled jacket with its torn lapels. 'I can imagine Gleeson might cling to his assailant to save himself from falling, but I'm damned if I can understand why the assailant should want to hold on to him!'

Jackson studied the tears for a few seconds, while the words used by the dead man and the gardener came back to him: ' . . . for one moment I was almost convinced it was an animal . . . all doubled up, it was, and ran close to the ground.' One of them might have exaggerated, perhaps, but it was impossible to discredit them both, especially since the evidence seemed to bear them out. Could it be that some unearthly monster like the vampires of old was responsible for this fiendish work? With a sharp admonition to himself for allowing his imagination to run away with him, he decided on the last explanation. One hint that motionless body had given him, however; but he intended to keep this to himself. Not that he was in the habit of keeping information back from his broad-minded colleague; only, this seemed something so indefinite that it might have to be abandoned altogether.

Next in their programme came the formal charging of Rogers. And when that was over, the butler being held on remand, Jackson and the two inspectors had their opportunity for interviewing him. This proved quite fruitless, however, the man sticking faithfully to his previous explanation. Searching questions concerning his relationship with the people in the manor, promises of lenience if he turned King's evidence, and conversely of stern impartiality, all met with the same response: a look of blank obstinacy.

'That's your story and you stick to it, I suppose?' cried the exasperated inspector at last, unconsciously lapsing into the lingo of American talkies.

'It's the truth,' the man declared stubbornly. 'And you couldn't make me tell you lies, not even to save myself from the gallows,' he added nobly. A little too nobly, for at this point Jackson, to whom all forms of pomposity seemed vaguely amusing, found himself smiling, and had to quickly compose his features in order that the fact should not become apparent to his companions.

'Unpleasant devil, isn't he?' remarked Charteris when they were again seated in the car, this time making towards the manor. 'Do you think he's holding anything back?'

The question was addressed to Jackson, and he thought for a few seconds before answering it. 'I'm inclined to believe he is,' he replied at length. 'Although I've no reason to think so, except that he's an unusually shifty piece of work; which being the case, of course he'd probably look guilty whether he'd anything to hide or not.'

'Everybody seems to have something up their sleeves in this case,' grumbled the inspector. And Jackson, knowing that he was referring to the instance of Frederick Gleeson, about which he still doubtless felt a little bit sore, forbore from making any retort.

Soon they were nearing their destination, and Jackson realised with a slight sinking feeling that he was fast approaching his ordeal with Lady Gertrude. He did not usually try to dodge the issue, but this business gave every indication of being so unpleasant that involuntarily his heart grew heavier at the thought of it.

Was it his imagination running away with him again, or had the beautiful manor taken on a more sinister aspect since he'd seen it last? When he'd come upon it for the first time yesterday, it had struck him as a serene and lovely place; but now it appeared grey and strangely forbidding, with the light summer clouds forming a fantastic pall above it as they threw the building into the shade. 'A house in the shadow of death' was the apt description he could not refrain from applying to it.

A mundane comment from the inspector brought him back to earth. 'Here we are,' declared that intensely practical and unimaginative personage as they swept up the tree-lined drive. 'And now for it!'

It's easy for him to say that when the brunt of the whole beastly business is going to fall upon me, thought Jackson as he brought the car to a standstill at the foot of the steps.

The party climbed out, and were just

turning towards the house, when they were arrested by a cry from Inspector Kennedy. Looking in the direction he was pointing, they all stayed where they were, as though rooted to the spot with amazement.

Through a gap in the hedge bordering on the drive came Ferguson, the gardener. Still hobbling, his face bore a look which seemed, even at that distance, to be an odd compromise between great sorrow and blazing anger. In his arms he was holding something very tenderly, although they could not at first make out what it was; and no sooner had he set eyes upon them than he began advancing with a slow, pathetic shuffle in their direction.

It was not until he was within a few paces of them that he spoke. 'I've been looking for you gentlemen,' he croaked in a voice that sounded like an echo from the tomb. 'I thought you was here to track down the killer for us?'

'So we are, Ferguson,' Jackson told him soothingly.

'Why don't you do your job properly, then?' the old man burst out passionately. 'Why don't you stop him? He's a devil, a fiend! He — he — ' For a second or two his voice broke, while the burning tears welled up in his eyes. 'He's taken my pal — the only pal I had. My Bob — my good old friend. Strangled him!'

With a pitiful gesture, he held up the thing he was carrying; and with a rush of sympathy, the three men recognised the lifeless form of his beloved collie. But before they could put their feelings into words, the old man's mood had changed again. Gone were the tears and the heartbreak, he now faced them as a raging fury!

'I'll get him, if you don't!' he stormed, raising his thin voice to its full extent. 'A life for a life, they say; and I'll kill him for this! Kill him! Kill him, I tell you!'

The quavering voice broke down completely, the tears welled up afresh, and with a choking sob the despairing old man tottered forward to be caught and held by the strong but friendly arms of Jackson and Charteris. But his words seemed to have been caught up by the breeze; they echoed in the trees, in the swish of the grass, in the rustle of the flowers: *I'll kill him for this! Kill him! Kill him, I tell you!*

Could they be a prophecy? Jackson asked himself thoughtfully; and as he looked at the grief-stricken old man beside him, he found it in his heart to wish that they were!

11

Hands that Kill!

'Poor old chap! He looks about all in,' remarked Charteris as he and Jackson entered the study. 'Leaving Kennedy to help him back to his cottage seemed about the only thing we could do.'

Jackson nodded as he dropped heavily into an easy chair. He was feeling badly shaken, for he knew it would be a long time before he'd forget that despairing look on Ferguson's face — if indeed he ever forgot it.

'To that old man, losing his dog was tantamount to you or I losing our best friend,' he said aloud. 'God! What sort of fiend is this creature prowling amongst us?'

'Whatever he is, I'll bet he's pretty strong,' retorted the inspector thoughtfully. 'Throttling a large dog like that's no child's play! I wonder how he did it?

Perhaps Kennedy'll be able to find out for us.'

Jackson agreed wearily; then, as though suddenly galvanised into action, he sprang to his feet. 'It's no use sitting here theorising,' he burst out sharply. 'We'd better do something.'

'What about Miss Harcourt, for a start?' suggested the inspector.

'Look — she's just crossing the lawn this minute.'

'I wonder what she's doing out there?' queried Jackson, joining his friend by the window. 'Oh, I see! She's been giving the child his lessons in the open. Good idea. Look out! She's coming in here!'

The two men stood back, one on either side of the windows, as the governess stepped hurriedly into the room. She was halfway across the floor when the inspector called out to her: 'Miss Harcourt!'

With a start and a look of frightened surprise, she turned. Her thoughts must certainly have been a very long way away whilst she was crossing the lawn, or she could not have failed to notice the two men. Her whole attitude showed, however, that she had not done so; this being the first intimation she'd received that she was under observation.

'Oh! What a shock you gave me, Inspector! And Mr. Jackson too!'

'I'm sorry, Miss Harcourt,' Charteris apologised as he and Jackson moved forward to meet her, 'but we were wondering if you'd mind answering a few questions.'

'Must I answer them now?' she demanded irritably. 'It's most inconvenient, you know. I'm just in the midst of giving Tommy a lesson.'

'Well, since you've found time enough to slip over here, Miss Harcourt,' Jackson put in courteously, 'I'm sure you've no objection to sparing a few more minutes for us?'

'I had to leave Tommy because I've unfortunately mislaid a most important book up in my room — at least, I think it must be in my room, for I can find it nowhere else. I was just going up to look for it,' she explained stiffly. 'Still, if I must be questioned, suppose I must! Perhaps you'll let me run upstairs first?'

'With pleasure.'

Without another look at either of them, she withdrew.

'Did you notice her eyes?' Charteris asked the moment after she'd gone.

'Yes. They looked as though she was brooding over something! Did you tell her about Gleeson's murder this morning?'

'No. Neither she nor the child were present. I expect the others have told her by this time, though.'

'Perhaps they have. But I wonder if the child knows?'

'I can answer that; he doesn't. Miss Gleeson said she thought it better to tell him his uncle had been unexpectedly called back to London.'

'A very wise precaution, too! That kid's had enough shocks for the present.' He moved back to the window and stood gazing out across the lawn to where he could just make out the figure of the child sitting with a book in the shade of a huge walnut tree. 'While we're waiting for Miss Harcourt,' he said over his shoulder to the inspector, 'I think I'll slip across and have a few words with the little fellow. You never know, he may have noticed something without quite realising its significance. Children are like that at his age, sometimes; and they're usually pretty observant too. Give me a call when you want me, will you?'

'Very well.'

Thrusting his hands deep down into his trouser pockets, Jackson sauntered off across the sun-drenched lawn.

As he approached him, the child looked up. 'Hello, Tommy!' Jackson called out cheerfully.

'Hello, Mr. Jackson!' the child responded, putting aside his book with an obvious sigh of relief.

'Good gracious!' Jackson exclaimed, sinking into the depths of a deck chair beside him, and at the same time observing the boy's pale features. 'What on earth's the matter with you? Haven't you been sleeping lately?'

'Oh yes, I've been sleeping all right. It's Bob. I've just seen Mr. Ferguson,' Tommy answered in a strained voice. 'He — he told me it'd been strangled. Is that true, Mr. Jackson?'

Jackson shook his head. 'No, I shouldn't think so,' he lied consolingly. 'The poor animal's not been well for some time. What are you reading?' he enquired, seeking to divert his youthful thoughts from so unpleasant a topic.

The child held up the book so that he could read the title.

'History? Rather a hot day for that, isn't it?'

'Yes, it is,' Tommy agreed heartily. 'But Miss Harcourt's in a bad mood this afternoon.'

'Why? What's wrong with her?'

'I don't know. But she's awfully cross about something.'

'Perhaps it's because she can't find that book of hers.'

'Oh no. She was grumpy long before that.'

'Really?'

'She says she can't stand it here much longer, and that she'll have to leave.'

'Does she?'

'Yes. I hope she doesn't mean it, though, because if she does, I shall be all by myself.'

As Jackson looked upon the forlorn little figure beside him, he felt a rush of sympathy. 'Oh no, you won't,' he told him comfortingly. 'Why, I shall be here for a little while longer, and I'll take you for some drives in the car. Would you like that?'

'Rather!'

'Good. It's a date, then. I must go now; there's the inspector beckoning to me. Cheerio, Tommy! And remember, that drive's a promise!'

On his way back to the house, Jackson became very thoughtful. Tommy and his rather pitiful plight had moved him strangely. *Poor kid*, he ruminated to himself. *Something must be done about him!*

The next moment, however, Tommy passed completely from his thoughts; for he had stepped through the French windows into the study, where the inspector and Miss Harcourt — the latter, book in hand — awaited him.

'Miss Harcourt wishes us to be as brief as possible so that she can return to her pupil,' Charteris explained as he entered.

'Why, certainly,' Jackson acquiesced. 'I

think it's most conscientious of Miss Harcourt, especially as she desires to leave.'

The shot went home. 'Who said I wanted to leave?' the governess snapped out savagely.

Jackson shrugged his shoulders. 'I can't remember offhand,' he answered carelessly. 'But you do, don't you?'

'I do not! I'm very happy here.'

'I'm glad to hear it; although I must confess to feeling a little surprised, considering all that's happened.'

'The tragic death of Sir James, if that's what you're referring to, Mr. Jackson, has done nothing to shake my loyalty to his family.'

'I never suspected it had, Miss Harcourt. Or the ... demise of his brother, either.'

'That didn't touch me. It took place outside the manor. I slept soundly last night, and knew nothing about it until I was told this morning.'

'But it must have upset you a little. You were acquainted with him, weren't you?'

'Only to say 'how do you do'.'

'Curious! He gave me to understand he knew you much better than that.'

Her eyes flickered slightly, but she made no comment.

'In fact, he told me all about a rather heated argument you'd had on the night Sir James died. But since according to his own account there was another witness present at the time, I can doubtless obtain corroboration from that quarter, if I wish.'

The governess eyed him with unmistakable contempt. 'If you're saying all this for the purpose of frightening me, Mr. Jackson, I'm afraid you're out to meet with a grave disappointment. I suppose you mean the stupid difference of opinion I had with Mr. Gleeson on the occasion when her ladyship was present? If so, I have only suppressed that out of consideration for her ladyship. You see, her brother-in-law did not show himself in a very pleasant light, to say the least of it!'

'Didn't he? And in what precise way did he appear to his detriment, Miss Harcourt?'

Eagerly he awaited her next words.

How was she going to get herself out of the awkward corner into which her admission had forced her? The next second, he knew.

'I'm sorry to say he was exceedingly drunk.'

So that was it! Hallucinations! The same weak explanation she and Lady Gertrude had offered to Gleeson himself.

'Can you oblige us with a detailed account of what took place between you on that night, do you think?' Charteris persisted, undaunted.

'Certainly I can, if you wish it.'

And she did give them a detailed account, then and there. It tallied with what Jackson had passed on to the inspector that morning, down to the minutest detail. All Gleeson's accusations against her were recorded faithfully, to the last word; all that was added, being her own explanation of his conduct, a transparent fabrication that convinced neither of her hearers. By the time she reached the end of her recital, they were even more suspicious of her than they had been at the start; an opinion they soon put into words the moment after she had left them.

'Well, what do you make of her, Jaggers?' enquired Charteris as the door closed behind her.

'Smart liar,' retorted that young man in no uncertain fashion.

'I entirely agree.'

At that moment, a heavy crunch on the gravel outside disturbed them. They both turned back to the window in time to witness the entrance of a very hot and exhausted Inspector Kennedy.

'What a job for a hot afternoon!' he complained as he sank into the nearest chair and mopped his streaming forehead. 'I've been with that old fellow, all this time.'

'How is he now?' asked Jackson.

'A bit quieter; but not much. It appears he found the dog lying in a ditch, on this side of the little gate that leads on to the road.'

'And it was on the other side of that little gate, just a few yards further up, that the body of Frederick Gleeson was discovered. Looks as though the murderer slipped through the gate and hid himself in the bushes until Gleeson's return.'

'Yes. But how did he find out Gleeson had gone to the village in the first place?' demanded the inspector. 'We all thought he'd gone to bed.'

'Maybe this person went to see him in his room, and found him missing.'

'Maybe. But coming back to the dog business again; I can't for the life of me understand why old Ferguson didn't hear the noise. The animal must have growled or something, or there would have been no object in killing it.'

'I think I can explain that,' Jackson began quietly. 'But in the first place, we must remember Ferguson was extremely tired. For one thing, he'd been having a fairly bad time with that foot of his; and also, he'd been disturbed once, earlier in the night, when Rogers tried to make his getaway.'

'The dog made enough noise then, in all conscience!'

'True. But in this case, the circumstances were slightly different. Let us take it then that the old man is in a deep sleep.

The murderer is creeping across the lawn, making for the gate. He comes through the trees, and then the dog spots him. As he slinks past, it begins to stalk after him. In this curious dark figure, the animal senses something uncanny. When they get near the gate, the murderer becomes conscious of the fact that he's been followed. He turns; the dog growls; he tries to increase his pace, but the animal springs upon him. By this time, they are some way from the cottage, so the sounds of the scuffle would be barely audible. As the dog jumps, the murderer catches him by the collar and throttles him!'

'That's Ferguson's theory too,' volunteered Inspector Kennedy.

'I expect you're right, Jaggers,' Charteris agreed. 'But I wish to God the ground had been soft enough to retain footprints! Great Scott, that fellow must be pretty useful with his hands, though! I shall be looking at everybody's hands from now on.'

'So shall I,' murmured Jackson softly. But the full significance of his words was lost on all but himself.

The booming of a gong sounded close at hand. Jackson glanced at his wrist watch. 'Two o'clock,' he exclaimed in surprise. 'Bit late for lunch, isn't it?'

'Perhaps some of them have been on an expedition,' the inspector suggested while the three of them moved towards the door. 'Anyway, let's have something to eat first and deal with Lady Gertrude afterwards, shall we?'

'That goes with me! I could do with a good meal,' Jackson admitted as they made their way out into the hall.

In the dining-room, the first person to be encountered was Joan. She seemed delighted to welcome the three of them to lunch. And soon, the others having arrived, they were all seated; 'all' consisting of Jackson and the two detectives; and Joan with her two suitors; Miss Harcourt and Tommy had elected to have their meal separately.

At first the atmosphere gave every promise of being extremely uncomfortable. But soon Jackson, with his easy flow of conversation, managed to liven proceedings up and persuade them to talk about their ordinary lives, as opposed to the grim realities of the present, which nobody could quite eradicate from their thoughts, try as they might.

Despite the continual nervous strain to which she was being subjected, Joan made a charming hostess and did all in her power to assist him in making things easy. As a matter of fact, it was on her account that the meal was so late, for she had spent the morning walking. Her reason for doing this, which she did not explain at the time, was primarily so that she might collect her scattered wits. For with so much to be done, so many arrangements to be made, she had need of all her faculties; especially since her stepmother seemed to have no intention whatsoever of shouldering her share of the burden.

The only reference made to the recent tragedy occurred when she enquired of Jackson if he'd broken the news to Lady Gertrude yet, to which he replied that he was going to do so immediately after lunch. The two men, Hoffman and Pat Burke, appeared to have spent the entire morning indoors; the former working on a transcription, and the latter writing the final chapter of one of his adventure sagas.

Thus, in liberal conversation upon these commonplace topics, the time passed pleasantly enough. And so interested had they all become, it was not until Joan rose from the table and announced her intention of retiring to her room to lie down that any of them noticed the abrupt change that had taken place in the weather. In an incredibly short space of time, the sky, which had been so bright, had become cloudy and overcast, while the atmosphere was charged with the vague mistiness that presages the coming of rain.

The meal over, Jackson first looked to the garaging of his car, and then he and Charteris made their way towards Lady Gertrude's room. Kennedy was left to interrogate all the other inmates of the establishment — including the servants, but with the exception of Joan and Miss Harcourt, and, of course, Tommy — concerning their movements on the previous night; a herculean task which, even if it proved unsuccessful, seemed likely to keep him occupied for the remainder of the afternoon. The reason for the exemption of Miss Harcourt was manifest, since she had already been questioned. And Joan had informed them before leaving the table that she had retired to bed at eleven-thirty on the previous night, and knew nothing more until the maid called her in the morning.

As they mounted the stairs, Jackson's sense of despondency deepened. He had long ago abandoned the idea of forming a detailed plan as to his course of action, and instead was now relying upon the inspiration of the moment.

They soon reached the room; and as the inspector raised his hand to knock, the first clap of thunder shattered the stillness, echoing hollowly throughout the old house as it quivered to its foundations. This was instantly followed by a vivid flash of lightning, while the inspector's fist descended upon the heavy oak panel in a loud and peremptory knock.

12

Tension

Unlike those downstairs, Lady Gertrude had witnessed the coming of the storm from its very earliest beginnings. Through the window of her room, she had watched the gathering clouds, feeling all the while that they symbolised the series of events that had so suddenly transformed her moderately quiet life into a seething maelstrom of conflicting emotions.

It was owing to her sheer incompetency to face these events that she had spent the past two days as a hermit, refusing to see anybody, even her stepdaughter. Nobody entered the apartment now, except the maid, who brought her meals. It was from this source that she had ascertained some of the details of Rogers's flight, although not a breath of news concerning the death of her brother-in-law had yet reached her. This was due to Inspector Charteris's foresight in warning the maid to say nothing about it.

So when the two men climbed the stairs to her room on that dreary afternoon, the bombshell they carried with them was of the most dangerous and highly explosive nature possible!

In answer to the imperative knock, she left her position by the window and unlocked the door, cautiously opening it a few inches.

'May we come in, your ladyship?' enquired the crisp matter-of-fact tones of Inspector Charteris.

With a little sigh of resignation, she stepped aside for him to enter. This attitude soon changed, however, when she saw who was accompanying him. For some reason or other, Lady Gertrude was very frightened of her nephew; in this respect, if in no other, Joan had been right in her estimation of her.

Closing the door, she stood facing them, rather like a hunted animal. 'Well, gentlemen,' she demanded harshly, 'what can I do for you?'

The inspector chose this moment at the very outset of the interview to place himself in the background; a position he occupied until the finish.

'Very little, I'm afraid, Aunt Gertrude,' Jackson began softly. 'Our reason for troubling you again is not solely for the purpose of questioning you; there is a far more serious motive behind it than that. In short, we are the bearers of bad news.'

The woman before him fixed her eyes on his enquiringly. Such a tragic figure did she cut as she stood there in the gloom, her pale, anxious features fitfully illuminated by the brilliant flashes of lightning, that he had hardly the heart left to perform what he'd set out to do. Looking at her quite dispassionately, it seemed impossible that any tragedy could befall her now to equal what had already passed.

Waiting for a clap of thunder to subside into a low distant growl, he took his courage in both hands and, after exhorting her to be brave — an exhortation which seemed peculiarly platitudinous under the circumstances — he told her as gently as possible the ghastly story he had come to impart.

She received it without a sound or a

movement. In fact, she remained so impassive that after a while, the two men began to doubt whether she had heard correctly. Then, without any warning, she tottered forward into Jackson's arms. Carefully they supported her to a chair, and she sank into it with a sigh of relief. Jackson flashed a meaningful glance at the inspector, the purport of which was plain, since he was hoping to be let off the remainder of his unpleasant task. But Charteris, either by accident or design, failed to respond.

'Are you feeling better?' he enquired solicitously.

Lady Gertrude nodded her head weakly, although the unhealthy purple hue of her lips belied the statement. Jackson made a particular note of this, remembering that it was usually the external accompaniment of a weak heart.

'Good. Now we're hoping you'll be able to help us.'

She raised her eyes and looked from one to the other of them. 'How?' she murmured so softly that they could barely hear.

'By telling us how you came to know *in*

advance that the murder was going to take place?'

The question, enunciated in clear hard undertones, had the effect of stupefying the woman to whom it was addressed. 'I don't know what you mean,' she answered.

'There, Aunt Gertrude, I'm afraid I must contradict you. You know only too well! Have you forgotten the words you were saying to Uncle Frederick last night, when I happened to be passing the door?'

'I have not. I refused to explain them to you!'

'That is a fact of which I am sensibly aware. Had you not done so, this later tragedy might have been averted.'

'You can't connect me with this horrible affair — ' she began wildly, when Jackson interrupted her.

'Oh yes I can,' he continued in the same relentless monotone. 'Before Uncle Frederick was murdered, he came to see me in my room at the Kentish Arms. Can you guess why he paid me that visit so late at night? Or must I tell you?'

'I've no idea.'

'Very well, I will tell you, then. He

came to give the details of what he'd seen on the night of Sir James's murder. Details, Aunt Gertrude, which you forced him to suppress.'

'And why shouldn't I force him to suppress such a ridiculous story?' she asked, rising from her chair.

'Wilful suppression of evidence — ' put in the inspector.

'Wilful suppression of evidence, nonsense!' she snapped at him. 'I merely desired to prevent Frederick from making a greater fool of himself than was necessary. The whole thing was a hallucination brought on, no doubt, by one of his drinking bouts. Miss Harcourt will tell you the same thing.'

'She has already told us the same thing,' Jackson continued smoothly, 'but it hardly accounts for the gardener having seen the black shape, too.'

'Ferguson saw it?'

'He did; only in running forward to catch it, he slipped and fell, so he missed seeing it enter Miss Harcourt's room. How do you account for that, if as you say, the whole thing was a figment of

Uncle Frederick's imagination?'

She looked at him with a scornful smile. 'I shouldn't dream of accounting for it,' she declared surprisingly. 'Why should I? On the one hand we have a drunkard, and on the. other an old man who's more than a little simple in the head. Who knows what flights of imagination they were capable of between them? I'm surprised that either of you should waste your time on such rubbish.'

'Are you suggesting that the fact that those two men saw exactly the same thing is mere coincidence?' Charteris demanded heatedly.

'Naturally,' came the serene reply.

'But that's preposterous, your ladyship, utterly preposterous!'

'Not at all, Inspector.'

'But — '

Jackson cut in on him. 'On that point, I'm in complete agreement with the inspector,' he said. 'It's quite unthinkable!'

'That's your opinion, gentlemen. I shall keep to mine.'

Never before had Jackson felt so completely nonplussed. This strange aloof

188

woman seemed to have no chink in her armour anywhere. She had an answer for everything, but never the one he'd hoped for.

'Is there anything else I can do for you, gentlemen?' her cold voice cut across his reverie.

His reply conveyed all the bitterness of spirit he was feeling. 'Nothing, since you've made up your mind to oppose us,' he told her. 'But remember this: those words of warning you spoke to Uncle Frederick before he was killed will have to be explained very soon. For when the murderer is found — and he will be, never you fear — your lack of co-operation now will most likely place you in the uncomfortable position of accessory in a murder charge. Good afternoon.'

With a stiff bow, Jackson turned towards the door, followed closely at his the heels by Inspector Charteris. As they let themselves into the passage, they heard the key grate in the lock behind them. Then out of the ominous stillness came the soft patter of raindrops, which in a few seconds developed into a torrential downpour.

At the foot of the stairs they encountered Miss Harcourt. She came flying out of the music-room, where she and Tommy had entrenched themselves, and rushed by them without so much as a backward glance. The reason for this strange behaviour was explained by Hoffman, who along with Pat Burke had been talking to them a moment before it happened. Apparently the governess had just laddered one of her stockings. And, since in her present mood anything was liable to infuriate her, she had rushed off then and there to change. A few seconds later she returned, however, in a more chastened frame of mind; so Charteris and Jackson had no choice but to return to the study, where they were eventually joined by Kennedy, whilst the other two adjourned to the lounge.

For those in the study, the remainder of the afternoon dragged by drearily. At a little after four, tea was brought to them; and for the space of a few minutes the atmosphere brightened, only to settle down to even deeper gloom immediately afterwards. The truth of the matter was that they all felt they had failed; Kennedy with his questioning which had yielded nothing, and the other two with Lady Gertrude, who still remained as deeply shrouded in mystery as ever.

To add to their depression, the rain persisted throughout the entire afternoon. And soon an odd sort of tension had begun to make itself felt amongst them; something that defied logic, but nevertheless grew as time wore on. It made itself felt at dinner also — a tedious enough meal, since Jackson, who had been responsible for lightening the conversation at the earlier repast, was this time in no mood to do so again.

Miss Harcourt and Tommy were there upon this occasion. The latter, although she vowed she'd taken half an hour's rest after tea, seemed to have suddenly become most alarmingly pale. And Hoffman looked as though all the cares of the world had descended upon him, for he had just received a trunk call from London summoning him to a business appointment on the next day that seemed likely to keep him well into the evening, thereby making it impossible for him to appear at the village concert as he'd promised.

Quite unexpectedly, Pat Burke, breaking off in the middle of a desultory conversation with Jackson about sport, offered his services as a modest deputy. He was, it seemed, something of a raconteur, and rather welcomed the opportunity for airing some of his newest anecdotes. Arrangements having been concluded very amicably, conversation once more languished; Jackson taking up his interrupted sports conversation, this time with Hoffman.

At last the time arrived for coffee and cigarettes, and they retired to the lounge. Here, the radio superseded conversation; and soon a typically English variety programme had begun to thaw the ice. Within a few minutes, loud guffaws from the men had taken the place of supercilious titters, and everything seemed more cheerful than it had been for some time past. Even Jackson found himself smiling — a state of affairs partly due to Joan, who, noting his depression, had forborne from asking him any questions about his interview with her stepmother.

Suddenly, in the midst of all this, Miss Harcourt uttered a stifled cry and slipped from her chair to the floor. Consternation followed: somebody immediately switched off the radio, while Charteris and Kennedy rushed to her assistance. Gently they lifted her to her feet. Her face had become ashen, whilst from between her white lips issued a low moaning sound.

'Miss Gleeson,' cried Charteris, 'would you mind showing us to her room?'

Joan stepped forward promptly. 'Of course not.'

'How about some brandy?' suggested Pat Burke's voice close at hand. But Miss Harcourt feebly shook her head.

'Ring up Doctor Meredith, Pat,' ordered Joan practically. 'This way, Inspector.' She preceded them out into the passage and up the stairs, as Pat Burke made his way to the phone.

With eyes grown large with wonderment, Tommy regarded the strange scene that was being enacted before him. Taking pity on the child, Hoffman drew him down onto the divan beside him and proceeded to talk kindly in a low monotone. The gist of his words was an assurance that Miss Harcourt was only a little faint and would soon be all right again. The child did his best to listen to this well-meant fabrication, but even he could not help being affected by the tension, which had now returned even more strongly than before.

For Jackson, this new development needed explaining; was it just an ordinary swoon, or was there something more behind it? He awaited the return of the two inspectors with impatience. As his eyes roved restlessly round the room, something bright on the carpet momentarily attracted his attention, and bending down, he picked the object up.

'Why, she's dropped her glasses!' he exclaimed to himself. Again his eyes sought the stairs, but still there was no sign of either Joan or the inspectors. A second later, Pat Burke returned, having eventually succeeded in getting hold of Doctor Meredith.

'He should be here in about fifteen minutes,' he announced.

'He lives somewhere in the village,

doesn't he?' asked Jackson, absentmindedly twirling the spectacles.

'Yes.'

By sheer force of habit and without thinking, Jackson slipped the spectacles on. Then he received a shock; for they were merely plain glass!

At first, the full significance of this discovery failed to strike him. But as soon as it did, he gave a gasp of surprise. Of course! Taken in conjunction with the recently dyed hair, what did it point to? A disguise! Silently he cursed himself as several kinds of an idiot for not realising the fact earlier.

'Good God! Whatever's happened, darling?'

These words spoken by Pat Burke drew his attention once again towards the stairs, in the direction of which the young man was hastily striding. The reason for his sudden exclamation was not far to seek.

Descending them, with Kennedy on one side and Charteris on the other, was Joan, her beautiful face the colour of marble. When they reached the hall, they gently handed her over to Pat; and the four of them advanced silently into the room.

At their entrance, Hoffman and Tommy instinctively rose to their feet. Gone beyond recall was the pleasant warmth of a few minutes ago, and in its place was a cold, chill feeling, like a breath from the tomb.

Inspector Charteris's voice, for once a little shaky, told them what they all wanted to know. 'I regret to inform you that Miss Harcourt is dead,' he announced simply.

A shudder went round the assembly, followed by a heavy oppressive silence, which was only broken by the monotonous dripping of the rain without, and the small, convulsive sounds of a child's sobbing . . .

13

Nightmare?

Inspector Charteris paced up and down the study, puffing irritably at his foul-smelling pipe, while Jackson sat in one of the easy chairs, a faraway expression in his eyes, and his mouth set in a thin hard line.

The unexpected demise of the governess, the last convulsive throes of whom the inspector had witnessed only a short time ago, had unnerved all of them, even the sturdy custodians of the law who were supposed to be inured to such things. Luckily Doctor Meredith, who arrived within a few minutes of the tragedy, happened to be the police surgeon; and it was for his verdict that they were now waiting.

Inspector Kennedy was with him, or rather standing by outside in case he should need any assistance, and at the same time doing nobly towards quieting the consternation that had broken out among the others.

So far, the servants had been kept in ignorance of this fresh development; a very wise precaution, since already more than half of their number had handed in notices, and servant worry on top of everything else was more than Joan could be expected to cope with. At the moment she was soothing Tommy, who had retired to bed in a state bordering on nervous collapse; a state of affairs for which Charteris held himself primarily responsible.

'Blamed fool!' he mumbled several times over in the course of his spasmodic peregrinations. 'I ought to have known better at my age than to scare a kid like that. But I'd clean forgotten about him, and that's the truth of it!'

'I don't wonder,' Jackson agreed wearily.

A light knock on the door brought Charteris to a standstill. 'Come in!'

The door opened to admit a handsome grey-haired man of middle age carrying a case. He was followed by Inspector Kennedy, and at their entrance Jackson rose to his feet.

'Well, Doctor?' enquired Charteris eagerly.

Doctor Meredith shook his head. 'I'm sorry to have to give you another problem to solve, Inspector,' he declared in his rather pedantic delivery. 'But I regret to say, Miss Harcourt has been poisoned.'

'I thought so!' Jackson muttered to himself. 'But why? Why?'

The doctor eyed him coolly. 'That is not my business to ascertain,' he retorted. 'But I gather from Inspector Kennedy that she was drinking from a coffee cup immediately before it happened. Now if I might suggest an analysis of that cup, it possibly — '

'Of course, Doctor, of course,' chimed in the inspector, who, in common with Jackson, gave the impression that he had suspected what the doctor's verdict would turn out to be all along. 'We can let you have the coffee cup all right. Kennedy,' he said, turning to the inspector, who had remained by the door, 'could you get that for the doctor? Oh, and you might find out from the servants whether the glass she was drinking out of at dinner-time has been washed up yet, or not. Do you think you could do that without arousing suspicion?'

'I'll do my best,' said Kennedy gloomily, turning on his heel. 'But the servants in this house are about as much at ease with me as mice are with a cat.'

As the door closed behind him, Charteris turned back to the doctor again. 'Have you any idea what particular poison it was?' he asked.

But the medical man shrugged his shoulders. 'It's difficult to say until I've had an autopsy,' he prevaricated.

'But if it was in her food, or something she drank,' the inspector continued thoughtfully, 'it looks as though the servants must be mixed up in it somewhere. Oh, of course, you'll want to phone, won't you?' The doctor had set eyes upon the telephone and was already crossing towards it. With a nod, he lifted the receiver.

He had barely concluded his arrangements when Kennedy returned carrying the coffee cup. 'Afraid this is all that's left,' he explained apologetically to the doctor, who advanced to meet him. 'Everything else has been washed up, as we expected.'

Carefully he handed the cup over to the doctor, who in his turn produced a small phial into which he poured the few remaining dregs of coffee; having stoppered this, he returned it to his case.

'How are the servants?' Charteris demanded of Kennedy as soon as this operation was over.

'In a state of complete panic,' replied the other shortly. 'No need to have warned me not to arouse suspicion; they're suspicious as a cartload of monkeys as it is! One of them saw the doctor arriving, and another saw Miss Gleeson trying to stop the little boy from crying as she took him up to bed. Wait until the ambulance arrives — we shall have some real fun then!'

The time they had to wait for the arrival of the ambulance seemed interminable. When it finally did pull up before the door, and the four men left the study to make their way out into the hall, the turmoil that had been long brewing burst upon them in all its pent-up fury.

The servants had arranged themselves in a chattering group in the middle of the floor, while the others were gathered together in the doorway of the lounge. The latter assembly included Joan, who, having, as she thought, soothed Tommy off to sleep, had returned to join the others.

The sight of the covered-up figure on the stretcher descending the stairs was all that it needed to send the servants into a complete state of the jitters, one of the parlour maids fainting upon the spot. It was in vain that Joan, supported in the background by the athletic figure of her lover, endeavoured to persuade them that there was nothing to be alarmed about. For there so obviously was plenty to be alarmed about! And it was a very petrified band of women who retired to the servants' quarters that night, one of them setting out on foot for the village within a few minutes of the departure of the doctor and the ambulance for Canterbury.

Things being once more restored to

normal, or as near normal as it was possible for them to be, the two inspectors and Jackson joined the others in the lounge, where Charteris, to whom all the unpleasant tasks seemed to be falling, informed them of the true cause of Miss Harcourt's death, ending up with an exhortation to all of them to come forward if they knew of anything likely to help him in his search.

But their blank expressions told him their own stories. Every soul in that room seemed mentally paralysed. Fear, or any strong emotion, for that matter, seemed to have worn itself out, leaving the inmates of Gleeson Manor numb to everything but a sense of being swept along by a series of fantastic and senseless hallucinations.

'Might I ask you something, Inspector?' said Joan, addressing Charteris as he finished speaking.

'Certainly, Miss Gleeson.'

'I — I hope it's not too much, but all these dreadful things that have been happening here have put all our nerves on edge. And I was wondering if you'd be so good as to stay the night?'

'Of course I will, if you wish me to. It's not strictly according to the rules for a Yard man to spend the night in the house, but I think, considering all that's happened, we might waive formalities for once. I should be delighted to stay, Miss Gleeson.'

'Thank you, Inspector.'

'Would you like me to keep you company, Inspector?' The offer came from Kennedy, and Charteris considered it for a moment or two before answering.

'No, thank you all the same, Kennedy,' he replied to the local man at length. 'What I would like you to do, though, is to come up first thing in the morning; then you can take over for an hour or so while I get a little sleep.'

'Just as you say!'

Joan glanced apologetically in the direction of Jackson. 'I would ask you to stay too,' she began, 'but — '

'I know,' he interrupted her, 'you don't like to go against her ladyship's wishes. I quite understand.'

'Tell you one thing,' said Charteris,

drawing her aside and whispering in her ear, 'I'd be very grateful if you could find me a plan of the house anywhere. It'd help me enormously in patrolling the passages.'

'I think there's one in Daddy's desk,' she replied. 'Shall I go and see?'

'If you will.'

Excusing herself to Hoffman and Pat, she preceded Jackson and the two inspectors towards the study.

After a little rummaging about in the drawers of the desk, she found what she sought: a comprehensive plan of the layout of the house. This she handed over to the inspector, who nodded his approval.

'And now, Miss Gleeson, I wonder if you'd do me just one more favour?' he urged, and she nodded immediately. 'Would you mind filling in the names of the persons occupying each of those bedrooms?'

'Of course I will, Inspector.' Without further demur, she took up a pencil and, seating herself before the desk, proceeded to do as he'd asked her.

'While Joan's doing that, don't you think it'd be a good idea if we took a look at Miss Harcourt's room?' said Jackson.

'An excellent suggestion,' Charteris agreed. 'Excuse us, Miss Gleeson; we'll be right back.'

Followed by Jackson and Kennedy, he mounted the stairs and led the way along the passage to where the door of the deceased's room stood open. They entered.

Despite their meticulous search, however, nothing came to light. The only point of interest lay in sheer absence of any personal belongings whatsoever — hardly any clothes, no letters, no photos, with exception of one on the table beside the bed; nothing that could help them even remotely in their estimation of the dead woman's character. The room seemed bare of everything but the bare essentials. And the end of a few minutes they were forced to give it up as a bad job.

As they were leaving, Jackson turned back and unobtrusively withdrew the photo from its cheap stand-up frame on the little table. For a few seconds he studied it intently, then he slipped it into his pocket and joined the others at the head of the stairs.

On reaching the hall below, they were greeted by a sudden inrush of cool air. It was explained by the fact that the front door stood half-open. Sensing no particular significance in this, they made their way back to the study, where they found Joan just approaching the completion of her task. In meticulous lettering she had filled in the name of each occupant in the little squares representing the bedrooms on the floor above. At their entrance she looked up.

'You don't need the servants' quarters filled in as well, do you, Inspector?' she enquired anxiously.

'No, thank you,' Charteris replied. 'That'll do splendidly.'

She gave a smile of relief. 'Thank the Lord for that,' she murmured as she rose to her feet.

'One minute!' Jackson called out after her as she moved towards the door. 'Have you ever seen this before?' From his pocket he withdrew the photo he had taken and held it up for her inspection.

'Of course I have,' she answered quickly. 'It's the enlargement of a snapshot I took of her myself.'

'How long ago was this?'

'About a month, I should think.'

'Judging by the expression on her face, Miss Harcourt wasn't exactly delighted with the idea of having her photo taken.'

'No, I'm afraid she wasn't. But she was quite sweet when I gave her that enlargement. You see — '

But the sentence was destined never to be concluded, for she was interrupted at this point by a series of screams accompanied by what sounded like a wild pattering of feet. In a flash the occupants of the study were out in the hall, and at the foot of the stairs. Down these, a wild dishevelled figure came running in their direction as though it were being pursued by a ghost. This figure, still uttering intermittent screams, they all instantly recognised as Tommy!

His eyes starting from their sockets, he came hurtling forward, seemingly oblivious of their presence until Jackson, who happened to be the nearest to him, caught the frantic child in his arms and swept him bodily off the stairs, setting him down amidst the group of startled spectators.

Joan, being the only woman present, naturally took charge of the proceedings immediately. And it was against her body that the child managed to put into something resembling coherent form the reason for his inexplicable hysteria.

While he was doing this, quite unobserved by the others, Hoffman slipped in from the garden.

'A man — all in black, Joan,' Tommy panted out wildly. 'He — he tried to climb in through the — window!'

In sharply defined contrast to the rest of them, Jackson stood watching this little scene with a curious look of abstraction. 'Kennedy!' he barked. 'The child's room — the front one on the right — see if anybody's up there!'

Scarcely waiting to hear the end of the order, Kennedy ran lightly up the stairs, taking two at a time, and disappeared from view.

'He — he was going to kill me, Joan — I know he was!' the child babbled inaudibly.

'There, there, dear,' murmured Joan, stroking his damp locks comfortingly.

'But I — I jumped out of bed and ran down here as fast as I could go!' he concluded, throwing his arms around her neck and crushing his body against hers, as though by so doing he could escape the horror that pursued him.

From his position at the foot of the stairs, Jackson still remained lost in thought.

'Not a sign of anybody up there, or in the garden either, so far as I could see,' boomed out the voice of Inspector Kennedy as he reappeared from above and ran down to join them.

'There's certainly nobody in the garden, Inspector. I could have told you that,' broke in the soft tones of Fritz Hoffman.

Charteris veered round on him suspiciously. 'How do you know?'

'Because I've only just come in,' the other replied simply.

'And you saw nobody?'

'Not a soul.'

'Where'd you been to?'

'To the garage, to have a look at my car.'

'What did you do that for, at this time of night?'

'You may remember, Inspector,' the musician retorted quietly, trying hard to keep control of his temper, 'that I have to go up to London in the morning. I haven't used my car for a few days, so I took this opportunity to see if it was in running order for tomorrow's journey.'

The inspector rounded unexpectedly on Pat, who had appeared in the doorway leading from the lounge. 'And where were you?'

'Why, in here of course,' the Irishman answered promptly, 'having a drink. Where else should I be?'

Before the inspector could answer this, another question had been forced on his attention. 'And what is the meaning of all this?' demanded a low vibrant voice close at hand.

On the instant all eyes were turned in the direction of the stairs, where, majestic as some monarch of old, stood Lady Gertrude! How long she had been there nobody knew, except perhaps Jackson; but her presence seemed in some indefinable way to add the finishing touch to all that had gone before.

Enquiringly, her eyes travelled from face to face, until they rested on Joan. 'Well?' she repeated, a note of anxiety making itself apparent in the cold voice for the first time.

'Nothing of importance,' Joan replied quietly. 'Tommy seems to have had a nightmare, that's all.'

'And is that any reason for turning the whole house into a bear garden?'

All at once Jackson came out of his trance and put one foot on the stairs. 'That alone would certainly not be sufficient reason, Aunt Gertrude,' he said in a hard, clear voice. 'But I'm afraid you're still in ignorance of all that has gone before. You see, with your room being situated where it is, it's quite natural that you wouldn't see the arrival and departure of the ambulance.'

'Ambulance?' The voice which echoed the words seemed to have already lost a great deal of its assertiveness, whilst her face had blanched visibly.

'Yes,' he continued callously. 'I regret to say we found it necessary to have Miss Harcourt removed.'

'Removed? What are you talking about? Why wasn't I told of this?'

'She had been poisoned!'

The pale hand that rested upon the banister gripped the woodwork convulsively. 'You mean, she's — dead?' she asked, having grown suddenly weak.

'Murdered would be a more accurate description.'

For the space of a few seconds, the old lady looked as though she might topple head foremost down the stairs. But with a supreme effort she pulled herself together. Slowly she turned on her heel. And as she did so, a wave of concern swept through the gathering below her. Sensing this, she glanced back at them over her shoulder. 'I am returning to my room,' she announced in a voice that still retained a great measure of its icy unapproachable dignity. 'And I do not wish anybody to accompany me. I want you all to understand that!'

It was a command, and as such left the

hearers with no course but to obey. Which they did unquestioningly, standing mutely by whilst the frail but regal figure of Lady Gertrude rounded the bend in the stairs and disappeared from their sights.

14

It Came Through the Window!

Her exit was the signal for a perfect babel of excitement as they all crowded into the lounge again. By now the child was recovering, and was prevailed upon by the inspector to recount his story afresh. This recital differed in no respect from what he had already told them, and everybody, with the exception of Charteris himself, was prepared to dismiss the whole thing as a nightmare.

But the fact that his pet suspect, Fritz Hoffman, happened to have been outside when it took place seemed rather too good a chance to lose, and in consequence he insisted upon examining the flowerbed beside the drainpipe which ran next to Tommy's bedroom, in the hope of finding possible footprints. Here he was disappointed, however, for the soil was obviously undisturbed.

Disgruntled, and feeling more than ever at a dead end, he returned to the house in time to see Joan once more escorting little Tommy up to his bedroom, and made his way with his two colleagues to their temporary headquarters in the study.

Here Jackson's preoccupation became more pronounced than before, and the inspector paused in the midst of a lengthy dissertation concerning the pros and cons of his suspicions of Hoffman, to enquire if he was listening. On being assured by Jackson that he was, he proceeded, and at the finish was greeted with a question about something totally different.

'Could you arrange for me to go to the Yard in the morning, do you think?' Jackson enquired innocently, taking advantage of the momentary silence.

Charteris raised a quizzical eyebrow. 'Why yes, if you want to,' he replied. 'But what for?'

'I want to see if I can identify this photograph of Miss Harcourt,' he explained, tapping his pocket.

'That's an idea! You think she's a crook, do you?'

'She might be.'

'In that case it'd be worthwhile for me to look into it myself, without worrying you.'

'No worry at all, I assure you. Besides, I'd rather do it if you don't mind.'

'Oh? Does that mean you've a theory?' asked the inspector, showing a gleam of interest for the first time.

'Yes and no,' Jackson said slowly. 'I have a theory, but it may well prove to be just a wild stab in the dark.'

'Aren't you going to let me in on it, Jaggers?'

The crime investigator shook his head. 'Afraid not, Charteris. I'm keeping it from everybody at the moment, even you. You see, I've no desire to appear a complete fool if it doesn't come off.'

'When will you know?'

'Tomorrow, if you'll give me your co-operation.'

'By arranging for them to assist you at the Yard?'

'That's it.'

'Right. I'll ring up first thing in the morning and see you get everything you want.'

'Thanks a lot, Inspector.'

'What time will you be starting out? Are you going by car?'

'Yes; I shall get going at about half-past seven.'

'Bit early for you, isn't it?' Charteris enquired chaffingly, remembering the other's weakness for lying in late. He turned his attention to Kennedy. 'What time's the earliest you can be here?'

'As soon as you like,' came the accommodating reply.

'Eight o'clock too early for you?'

'No.'

'Then I'll ring up the Yard at eight o'clock, Jaggers, just before I go off. That do all right?'

'Splendid!'

'And if your theory proves correct, what do I get out of it?'

Jackson fixed him with a clear, determined glance. 'The murderer; whose reign of terror is, I think, drawing to a close,' he said softly.

'Well, Jaggers, I've never known you to exaggerate, so I'll possess myself in patience until you return. And good luck!'

'Thanks.'

Jackson rose from his chair. 'Before I go, may I have a look at that plan?'

'Sure.'

Making his way to the desk, he studied it for several moments in silence.

'Found what you want?' the inspector asked as he straightened himself up.

'Yes, thanks. I think I'll be getting along now, if you don't mind. How about Inspector Kennedy? Can I give you a lift anywhere?'

The local inspector looked towards the Yard man enquiringly.

'You get along, Kennedy,' Charteris told him affably. 'You'll need some rest if you're going to be back here at eight.'

'Thank you, Inspector.'

With a 'good night' to Charteris, the other two moved towards the door, when Jackson stopped.

'One thing I'd like to mention, Charteris.'

'What's that?'

'Watch everybody's hands.'

'Because of the scratches on Gleeson's body?'

'Yes. The person who made those must have had exceptionally long nails.'

Charteris surveyed his own short ones critically.

'I worked that out too!'

'And you never told me!' Jackson laughed. 'We're beginning to have secrets from each other; that'll never do!'

'Well, I'm safe enough on that score,' retorted the inspector, holding up his hands. 'How about you?'

'Not so good,' Jackson admitted, hiding his slim well-kept hands in his pockets. 'But at least mine are decently manicured. What about yours?'

He turned to where he had expected to find the familiar figure of the local inspector, but Kennedy had already passed out into the hall; determined, no doubt, to take Charteris at his word and get every minute of respite that was coming to him.

Remarking lightly upon this, Jackson left the study and turned in the direction of the front door. Before reaching this objective, however, he observed a light coming from the half-open door of the lounge, and put his head round to bid the occupants good night.

Scarcely knowing how to pass the time, yet with a curious antipathy towards the idea of moving into another room, Joan, Fritz and Pat were all seated round the open fireplace indulging in a fitful conversation. At Jackson's cheery good night, they looked up, and there was an expression of genuine regret on each of their faces. It was a great compliment to his personal charm that he had succeeded in making himself so popular with them, despite the fact that he was unofficially investigating the cause of the murders; a position which, meritorious though it might be from the point of view of justice, was scarcely conducive to a feeling of friendliness between himself and his unfortunate suspects.

The assurance that he had won through with them, so to speak, was put into words the moment after he'd left, by Pat Burke. 'Nice chap, that!' he said in his typically straightforward manner. 'I only wish I could meet him under pleasanter circumstances.'

'Perhaps you will, darling — later on,' suggested Joan in a soft little voice, while Pat pressed her hand gently where it lay on the settee beside him.

'Are you thinking of asking him to give you away, by any chance, Joan?' Hoffman asked her with a charming smile.

His answer was in the wistful expression that immediately filled her eyes.

'I might have known it,' he continued in the same pleasant tone. 'May I hope I shall be invited to the wedding also?'

'Of course, Fritz,' Pat hastened to set his mind at rest on the point.

'I'm afraid we misjudged you, my dear,' Joan admitted generously, stretching out her free hand towards him.

Rising to his feet, Hoffman took it in his and kissed it; a sincere tribute, robbed of any trace of theatricality by the simplicity with which it was performed. 'That's very gracious of you,' he said in a voice grown unexpectedly shaky. 'And now I think I'd better retire.'

'Must you?' asked Pat, and the light in his eyes bore witness to his genuineness.

'I have to be away early in the

morning,' the musician explained, 'so I must. Good night to both of you, and — and many thanks!' In an effort to hide his emotion, he turned smartly on his heel and left the room.

'He's a dear thing, really,' said Joan, inclining towards her lover. 'I ought to feel frightfully honoured that he deigned to look at me at all.'

'Talk like that and I shall be getting jealous.'

She smiled; a wholly enchanting transformation revealing the even line of her white teeth. 'That would be silly of you,' she admonished Pat tenderly, meeting his ardent gaze.

'Would it?' his voice had become as intimate as her own, and the palm of his hand was in contact with the delicious warmth of hers.

'You know it would — or if you don't, then you ought to.'

'I do, darling, but I can't think what I've done to deserve so much.'

'Or I. I know millions of people have said being in love's wonderful before; but it is, isn't it?'

'Being in love with you, dearest, seems just like paradise to me!'

Their hands now clung together, as did their lips. Though the shadow of death and terror might hover over Gleeson Manor, it was quite powerless to blight this strong youthful love of theirs which, in the proverbial way that so seldom comes true in real life, seemed to thrive on adversity.

The thrill of that kiss lingered with Joan long after they had parted for the night. And as she stood alone in her room, after dismissing her maid, her sensitive fingers sought her lips, as though unable to believe such ecstasy could really be hers. Caressingly she pressed her hands against her cheeks.

It was then she detected a slight abrasion she hadn't noticed before. Looking at her hand under the shaded lamp on her dressing-table, she gave a little gasp of surprise.

'Good heavens! Whyever didn't I see that before?' she exclaimed.

Slightly livid against the olive skin of the back of her hand, there appeared a long scar.

Unlike the former occasion, when he had found it necessary to drive from Gleeson Manor down to the Kentish Arms with a demoniacal chuckle ringing in his ears, Conway Jackson found the present journey passed pleasantly enough. The reason for this could be chiefly attributed to his companion, Inspector Kennedy, whose cheerful company would have been capable of dispersing untold numbers of spooks and suchlike, had it been called upon to do so. In him, Jackson had certainly found a real godsend!

After getting the Alvis out of the garage from between Hoffman's palatial tourer and Pat's old-fashioned four-seater, they took the lonely country road for Hamlin Hollow. Conversation, as might have been expected under the circumstances, naturally turned upon the case of the moment. And Jackson was surprised to learn that Kennedy did not share in Charteris's ill-founded suspicions of Fritz Hoffman. On the other hand, though, he admitted frankly that he could advance no alternative theory of his own. Judging by what he said, he appeared to harbour an intensive form of hero-worship for Jackson. And it was on account of this that he was patiently biding his time, in the expectation of some stunning declaration from that quarter which would provide a solution to the whole business.

Gradually their conversation drifted by easy stages to the more recent tragedy of Miss Harcourt. But here, it seemed, they were both baffled. That she had been poisoned was now an established fact, but unless the coffee dregs produced something, it seemed practically impossible to ascertain in what way the fatal dose had been administered. This was a problem that had been worrying Jackson considerably until the last half-hour or so. It was during this period that he had received the inspiration which, if correct, might signify the finish of the dramatic happenings at Gleeson Manor. If wrong, though, it meant he would have to start his deductions all over again from the very beginning; a proceeding which at this stage appeared extremely distasteful to him.

So preoccupied were they with their discussion that the lights of the Kentish Arms were sighted before they were aware of how quickly the time had passed. Having offered to take Kennedy further on his way — a suggestion that was courteously rejected, the inspector vowing that he lived within easy walking distance — Jackson drew to a standstill before the inn and parted from him. At first, he had toyed with the idea of asking the man in for supper; but remembering he had one or two details to think over for his campaign of the morrow, he dismissed it, and contented himself with watching the sturdy figure of the police officer swinging away along the deserted high street.

At the side door he was greeted this time by the proprietor himself, who supervised in person the locking up of his car for the night. Whilst they were doing this, the ex-pugilist kept up a ceaseless barrage of hearty small talk. But when they reached Jackson's room, he announced his intention of retiring; an intention his guest showed no inclination to discourage.

As the man turned to go, Jackson noticed for the first time that he had just the suspicion of an ugly black ring round his left eye. He had no opportunity of commenting upon this, for at that moment Judy appeared with his steaming supper. Seeing her friendly look, he hadn't the heart to tell her that it was rather a hot night for beefsteak pudding, but prepared to tuck into it.

'You're looking tired tonight, Judy,' he observed when she returned with the teapot a few minutes later.

'I'm not, really,' she said, striving vainly to cover up the listless expression of her eyes with a bright smile. But Jackson was not to be taken in so easily.

'Oh yes, you are,' he contradicted her. 'Now you run straight off to bed.'

'But — but who's going to lock up?' she asked disappointedly, seeking for some excuse that might bring her another invitation to partake of tea, as on the previous night.

'I'll see to that,' he said, deaf to her tone of entreaty.

'Will you? Thank you, sir,' she replied

weakly, seeing she was beaten.

'Oh, by the way, if it's not a personal question, how did your father get that black eye?'

She turned immediately, sensing an excuse to stay for a few minutes, anyway. 'One of the men in the public bar got a bit rough, and Dad had to throw him out,' she explained.

'Pretty nasty eye he's got.'

Judy permitted herself a slight giggle. 'You should see the other chap,' she told him.

'I'd rather not, if it's all the same to you,' Jackson retorted with a laugh. Then, before she could say anything further, 'Well, have a good night's sleep.'

'I will. Thank you, sir.' Her opportunity gone, and with no other excuse to hand, she sulkily withdrew.

The moment he was alone, the preoccupied expression that had been in such evidence at the manor returned to Jackson's face again. It remained throughout the meal — or rather, throughout as much of it as he could digest; for he was now like a hunter on the trail, and even eating and drinking seemed a senseless waste of time until he had laid his quarry by the heels.

It was not until he rose to lock up that he remembered he had given no instructions as to what time he was to be called in the morning. Hastily scribbling a note, he placed it in the most prominent position he could find on the hall table.

'These country people are sure to be early risers,' he conjectured to himself. 'And even if they're not, I've the good old alarm to wake me.' An alarm clock was always his indispensable travelling companion.

Seeing that Judy had taken the precaution to lock up herself, not trusting him to do so, he went back to his room; and although it was only a few minutes after eleven, an early hour for him, he prepared to retire. Last thing before turning in to bed, he threw wide the window; for strange to say, the recent rain seemed to have done little towards relieving the heat, the weather being still as sultry as ever. Having done this, he switched off the light, and slipped between the sheets.

Tired though he was, sleep refused to come, and for over an hour he tossed about restlessly. Although he was only covered by a sheet, the heat seemed insufferable. And at last, in desperation, when the illuminated dial of the clock beside his bed proclaimed that it was half-past twelve, he sat up preparatory to getting out of bed to fetch himself a cigarette. It was a lucky thing for him that he did; otherwise that night might well have been his last!

Something drew his eyes towards the open window — and then he saw it! Sharply defined against the opaque gloom outside could be distinguished an ugly black form. In the velvety stillness, Jackson's heart seemed to miss a beat. The vampire man! For the space of a few seconds his brain began to panic; then, as though he had received a shower of cold water, his thoughts suddenly became lucid again.

The first point he realised was that although he could see the thing at the window, it could not see him — yet.

Already it was climbing over the sill, so he knew his advantage was but a momentary one. Silently he cursed himself for having left his automatic in his suitcase across the room, as he slipped from the bed and flattened himself against the wall ready to spring.

With uncanny silence, the figure — now inside the room — crept forward. The carefully guarded beam of a torch cut through the blackness, to fix itself upon his suit, where it hung neatly on its hanger behind the door. The next instant the light went out!

Jackson held his breath until it hurt. The reason for the torch being flashed upon his clothes became abundantly clear, for now the intruder was assured that he had entered the right room. Slowly the figure turned in the direction of the bed; with animal stealth it advanced towards it . . . cautiously . . . step by step . . . inch by inch. It was now poised over the bed, its back towards Jackson. His moment had come. Without a sound, he sprang upon it!

A low growl of surprise burst from it as

they engaged in a fierce struggle. Not a sound broke the stillness apart from their short stabbing breaths whilst they rocked to and fro in a death-like embrace.

There was something horrifying about it. Never had Jackson met such an opponent before! It was like fighting with some terrible and elusive shadow. One moment it seemed within his grasp; the next it had darted back far beyond his reach.

At last, however, after what seemed an eternity, their bodies met for the second time. With a crash they fell to the floor, bringing the table with them — Jackson underneath. He experienced a sickening thud as his head struck the boards . . . a blaze of stars danced before his eyes . . . then, blackness; deep and impenetrable . . .

★ ★ ★

Somebody was bathing his burning forehead with something cool. A murmur of voices sounded near at hand. Slowly he opened his eyes, but the instant pain this simple action provoked caused him to close them again immediately — though not before he had seen Judy's anxious face bending over him, and had realised that he was lying safely in his bed at the Kentish Arms.

A few minutes later he roused sufficient strength to speak. 'What — what happened?' he asked weakly.

Judy's voice, grown strangely soft and maternal, floated to him across what seemed a limitless distance. 'We found you lying on the floor, unconscious,' she was saying. 'We'd heard a crash upstairs — it must have been the table falling over — and Dad came down to see what was wrong.'

'Did you — see anybody else?' he persisted.

'No, sir,' answered another voice, a man's this time. 'He must have climbed out of the window — though there wasn't any sign of him in the lane.'

'So he — got away, did he?'

'Yes, sir. But don't you worry, sir, the police will get him for you!'

'Will they? I wonder!' All at once he thought of the proprietor's beefy fists, and a wave of regret swept through his numbed brain. 'I — I wish you could have — caught him, though,' he murmured disjointedly.

Gradually, with great difficulty, he managed to open his eyes and fixed them on the faces before him. He could make out two now, the proprietor's and his daughter's. He was just on the point of saying something to them, however, when darkness once again descended upon him; and he suddenly felt himself falling, as though into a bottomless pit . . .

15

Recognition

The light from the study cut across the lawn like a knife. Tonight no moon shed its gentle radiance over the spacious grounds of Gleeson Manor; everything was black as pitch.

With a yawn, Inspector Charteris stretched himself and took several paces up and down the square of carpet. Up till the present, the night had proved tedious. Every half hour he had patrolled the passages on the ground and first floors, but so far nothing untoward had revealed itself. Taking his pipe from his pocket, he filled and lighted it, returning to his seat beside the stone fireplace.

As he puffed away, his thoughts automatically turned once again to his case against Fritz Hoffman, and at great length he proceeded to itemise the pieces of evidence that had found their way into his possession. Most important of these, of course, was the motive he had had in the initial case of Sir James. But was it strong enough? Because the unfortunate baronet had at last acceded to his daughter's request that she might become engaged to Pat Burke, was he rousing such an unnatural hatred in the other's breast that nothing could allay it, short of the sacrificing of a life? And even if it were so, surely the person to suffer should have been the hated rival, Pat Burke, and no other?

As these points passed through his brain, the inspector shook his head dolefully. Although he had clung on to this theory tenaciously, as a drowning man might to a straw, he was far too intelligent to overlook its palpable deficiencies. No, it looked as though his case had fallen to the ground.

Of one thing he was certain, however, and that was that all three murders were the work of the same hand — an inside hand at that. This fact was borne out, moreover, by the killing of the dog, which had evidently stood in the path of the murderer when he was getting from the grounds to the road, where he had planned to lie in wait for the return of the hapless Frederick Gleeson.

This naturally narrowed down the list of suspects considerably; but it also led to a cul-de-sac so far as the inspector was concerned, for it brought him once again face to face with that ugly problem of a motive. And so far as he could see, discounting Fritz Hoffman, none of them appeared to have the least reason for wishing the old man dead. On the contrary, it seemed to their advantage to have him living.

This definitely applied in the case of Pat Burke, who, having obtained Sir James's consent to his engagement, must have felt a genuine sense of affection for his future father-in-law. It must apply equally to Joan. And that brought him to Lady Gertrude.

Could it be possible that this mysterious woman, instead of merely shielding the criminal, as they already suspected, was in reality the criminal herself? Gleeson's tale discredited that view, for if she had killed her husband it would have been impossible for her to have reached her room in time to prevent her brother-in-law from forcing an entrance into Miss Harcourt's. Besides, had she been the culprit herself, then Gleeson's story of the figure swarming up the drainpipe would have to be taken as a hallucination. In which case, her determined effort at preventing him from entering Miss Harcourt's room would have been entirely pointless, there being nothing inside for him to discover.

Viewed from this uncompromising angle, the whole affair looked gloomy enough indeed! He felt as though he hadn't even begun in his search — hadn't even come across the signpost that would direct him along the right avenue.

It was at such moments as these that the inspector would have cheerfully given his all for that peculiar intuitive faculty Jackson had been born with gratis. But such gifts are not to be purchased. Inspector Charteris was, and would remain till the end of his days, a hardworking and thoroughly competent police officer; but never would he be able to marshal that curious awareness that is the perquisite of the born criminologist. It says much for his fund of common sense that he realised this fact early on.

A hasty glance at his heavy gold watch informed him that it was half an hour since he'd last patrolled the passages, and he rose eagerly to his feet. In spite of the oppressive atmosphere, he still felt wide awake, and each time he made his circuit of the building he was filled with fresh expectancy. So far, as has been remarked before, this had proved quite unfounded. But hope springs eternal! And so on this occasion, as on the former ones, he set out in a spirit of buoyancy and optimism.

He had already reached the door when a sound came to his alert ears that caused him to pause, and when it was repeated, stop dead in his tracks. The faintest indication of a foot crunching on the gravel outside was all his trained faculties had detected, but it was sufficient to result in all his senses becoming tensed up in less than a second.

Stepping lightly on his toes, he made

his way round the desk. With a little click, he switched out the reading lamp, and the room was immediately swallowed up in complete and unrelieved blackness. This time, unlike upon a similar occasion, only two nights ago when the hand of a murderer had extinguished the same lamp, no tell-tale streak of moonlight found its way through a crevice in the curtains, no breath of wind disturbing the deceptive solidity of their still folds.

For the space of a few seconds, Charteris remained where he was. Then, so softly that it might easily have been overlooked altogether, he heard it again. Crunch . . . crunch . . . With incredible agility in one of such massive proportions, the inspector circled round the desk and felt his way to the centre of the curtains. Behind them, the French windows were unlatched and a little apart; he'd seen to this himself earlier, in case of such an emergency as the present. Slowly, cautiously, he slipped out between them into the dark garden beyond.

At first it seemed as black as in the study. But appearances being often deceptive, he found when his eyes were accustomed to the gloom that things within the radius of a few feet became barely visible. And as another crunch broke the stillness, this time slightly nearer and louder than before, the dim shape of a man moved haltingly in view.

Flattening himself against the window, Charteris waited for it to come closer. Slowly, painfully, the seconds ticked by, as, with infinite care, the figure moved in his direction. At last, when it was almost within arm's reach, he took a deep breath and hurled himself upon it!

The result turned out to be short, sharp and decisive. The man, thus startled, landed out savagely with some heavy implement he was carrying. After receiving one nasty crack on the elbow, Charteris managed to keep clear of this. And then, seeing his opportunity, he jumped in, delivering his opponent a short right to the jaw. The man lost his footing and staggered backwards as with one swift movement the inspector wrenched away the implement that had been wielded against him with such unpleasant results. Throwing this to the ground, he followed up his advantage by smartly pinioning the man's arms to his sides and marching him briskly forward into the study.

Throughout this formidable contest not a word had been spoken, so it was quite understandable that the sleeping household remained undisturbed. Disengaging one hand, the inspector fumbled with the little knob on the reading lamp, and the next moment it came on. Tilting the shade so as to see his prisoner more clearly, he focused the light from the naked bulb full onto the man's face.

'Great Scott! What on earth are you doing out at this time of night?' he let out explosively.

Ferguson, finding his hands suddenly released, fingered his chin ruefully. 'Lookin' for *him*!' he muttered thickly. Then, turning to his captor: 'I hope I didn't hurt you, Inspector?' he said with genuine concern.

The inspector felt his elbow. 'Not your fault if you didn't,' he growled ungraciously. 'What in heaven's name were you carrying?'

'My gun, sir,' the other replied promptly. 'I use it against poachers.'

'Well, thank the Lord you didn't get a chance to use it against me!'

'You were too quick for me, sir.'

'That reminds me — how's your chin? I'm afraid I hit you pretty hard.'

'I'll have a bruise there the size of an egg in the mornin'.'

'Well, you've only yourself to blame, you know. Why didn't you tell me you were going to do a spot of unofficial patrolling in the grounds?'

'Never thought of it, sir.'

The inspector winced. 'Been better for both of us if you had,' he retorted. 'I daren't look at this arm of mine for fear it's broken. Here, give me a hand — you did it!'

Carefully, with the help of the gardener, he removed his jacket and rolled up his shirt sleeve to reveal an ugly purple patch, just above the elbow. Ferguson coloured as he saw it, and made a few stammering apologies before the inspector cut him short.

'What can we do about it?' he

demanded brusquely. 'Put your hand in the right side pocket of that jacket over there, and you'll find a handkerchief.'

The gardener obediently followed out his instructions, and the handkerchief was produced.

'Now pour some of that water into the glass, and soak it.' He pointed to where a decanter of drinking water stood with a tumbler at the side of the desk. The handkerchief duly moistened, it was bandaged round the bruised forearm.

'Do you want your jacket on, sir?' Ferguson enquired, now eager to do all in his power to make amends.

Charteris shook his head. 'No, thanks. I feel more comfortable like this.'

'Then I can get back to my job, sir.' The voice of the old gardener had once more become grim, and the inspector looked at him in surprise.

'After that jab on the jaw, I should have thought you'd have been making tracks for bed.' One look at the expression on the old man's face was sufficient to show that it was quite useless to argue with him, so Charteris gave it up as a bad job.

'Very well,' he said shortly. 'It's your business, I suppose. It's about time I made my circuit of the passages.'

'Good night, sir.'

'Good night, Ferguson. And mind you don't kill yourself with that popgun of yours.'

But the remark was received with no answering smile by the white-haired man, who turned back towards the window. His eyes, which a moment ago had known the softening light of sympathy, were now hard as stones and curiously bright.

Passing out into the garden, he had no trouble in finding his gun, which lay a few feet away from where they'd been struggling. And picking it up, he began to move slowly forward, taking special care this time to keep on the grass, which muffled his footsteps.

Approaching the corner of the house, his instincts at once sharpened, and his slow progress became more cautious than ever. Eventually he turned the bend and advanced along the side of the house. Ahead loomed the back of the garage.

Then, in the shadows, he detected

something! At the foot of the drainpipe that ran up beside the open window of Joan's bedroom, there crouched a sinister black figure!

Nervous of making a second mistake, the old man crept forward softly, taking care as he did so to bring the rifle up to his shoulder in readiness to fire. But it was his one fatal mistake — his slowness proved his undoing.

The figure, which had already begun its ascent up the drainpipe, saw him, and acted unhesitatingly. Without making a sound, it jumped, landing on the gardener and hurling him to the ground, his gun sent flying from his grasp. What followed was a life and death struggle. Unable to rise, the old man fought with all the strength of his already weakened resources. But the result was a foregone conclusion.

With horrifying certainty, those soft death-dealing fingers found their way to his frail old throat. The gentle pressure increased until his eyes began to start from his head, his face turning from purple to black as the precious life-giving oxygen was throttled from his body.

At one moment, before darkness descended upon him, he had the doubtful privilege of glimpsing his opponent's features. Doubtful, for although he recognised them, as his look of surprise betokened, he was not destined to live to make use of his dangerous knowledge.

It was only a matter of a few moments before the end came. And the old gardener was engulfed by the final darkness, which, in its place, speedily gave way to an assuaging oblivion . . .

★　★　★

Joan was generally what might be termed a deep sleeper; yet on this particular night she felt strangely restless. The heat may have been responsible for this in part, and also the disturbing events of the past two days, which had been enough to upset anybody. These reasons doubtless accounted also for her tangled dreams — but they could not be held responsible for what directly followed.

Having managed to doze for a little while, she slowly opened her eyes as the last remnants of sleep withdrew themselves from her. She felt resentful against somebody — she didn't know quite who — for disturbing her. And it was while she was still in this frame of mind that she glanced idly round the darkened apartment.

Suddenly she was wide awake — alive in every nerve. What had caused this sudden transition from semi- to complete consciousness, it was impossible to say. She had seen nothing. The outline of the window, standing open against the dim night outside, showed up indistinctly across the floor; the familiar objects, such as the dressing-table, chairs, and low divan also came into view as her eyes grew accustomed to the darkness. Everything seemed as it had always been; nothing altered.

There was only one portion of the room, for it was not a very large one, which she was unable to see — and that was the space immediately around her bed. An odd bristling, rather like electricity, began to make itself felt at the nape of her neck. Should she venture a glance over the side? With a burst of bravery, she was about to sit up with this end in view, when the necessity for such a course became superfluous. Something black slipped out of the darkness and began to travel sinuously over the bedclothes.

She lay watching it with the same kind of hypnotic fascination as one might experience when looking at a reptile. The slim black thing soon proved to be an arm; and it was quickly followed by another, which in its turn was superseded by a dark indistinguishable body that drew itself along the bedclothes beside her.

By this time her powers of speech had deserted her. And although she dearly wanted to scream, she could not even emit a hoarse croak, for her throat seemed to have become paralysed on the instant. Bereft of speech, she lay quite still, the cold sweat of fear clinging in icy drops all over her body. Something, some inner sense, warned her to stay where she was. And displaying faith in her intuition, such as few men but a great number of women possess, she did as her spirit dictated, and closed her eyes.

The figure had now ceased moving, and a hot unsavoury breath fanned her cheeks. But still she showed no signs of wakefulness.

Out of the blackness slipped a tentative hand, the flabby fingertips of which caressed her closed lids. A slight grunt of satisfaction reached her straining ears. Then the fingers were withdrawn. What now? she asked herself.

The body that was pressed against her felt repellently soft, like the fingers had done. Something was happening! She could not tell what it was without opening her eyes, and that she dared not do. Was it her imagination, or was that burning breath drawing nearer? She felt sure it was! Did that mean she was going to be killed, then?

She parted her lips ever so slightly, and something brushed against them; something moist. She held her breath in horror as a wet, greedy mouth sought hers. Desperately she strove to suppress the shudder of revulsion which bade fair to run through her limbs, at the same moment as the soft, flaccid lips deposited a light but incredibly obscene and sensual kiss upon her own.

By this time her mind was in such a state of chaos that she was scarcely aware of the stealthy withdrawal of the soft thing from beside her. The slight sound of padded footfalls did not reach her either as she lay, her whole body twitching convulsively with a terror that she found herself powerless to control.

Even the slight click of the door failed to rouse her. And it was not until several seconds later, when she discovered she was alone, that realisation came to her in a rush and she jumped wildly from her bed. If it had been dark before, it was even more so now; and the pattering from outside the window bore witness to the fact that the rain had returned in double force.

This meant nothing to Joan, however, as she staggered blindly across the floor. Reaching the door, she threw it open and hurled herself into the passage beyond. It was then, and not until then, that she found her voice; and scream after ear-splitting scream rent the stillness of the night!

As though from nowhere, Inspector Charteris appeared at the head of the stairs, placing himself directly in the course of her frenzied flight. The next second she had cannoned headlong into him with a scream!

16

Suspicions Confirmed

Looking back upon the case in future years, Charteris decided that the rain which fell that night, while he was hearing Joan's story and thinking of descending to the garden to search for footprints, was typical of the whole affair.

The screams had aroused the entire household — even Lady Gertrude joining in the eager throng that flocked at the inspector's heels, avid for an explanation of the strange disturbance.

As soon as Joan had recovered sufficiently, she told them her inexplicable story. But far from assisting towards the elucidation of the mystery, it merely deepened it, baffling everybody, including her stepmother.

When questioned as to their whereabouts at the time of the outrage, they all, without a single exception, produced the same unsatisfactory alibi of having been asleep. After a few vague attempts at probing this, the inspector gave way and let them return to their beds again; a dismissal which none of them were slow in accepting.

Joan, being a very courageous young woman, elected to spend the remainder of the night in the same room; whilst the inspector, having been foiled by the elements in his intention of searching for footprints, returned with his arm in an improvised sling to his solitary vigil in the study.

Thus it came about that the body of Harry Ferguson was not discovered until the following morning, when it was brought to light by a terrified parlour maid. Going into the garden before breakfast for the purpose of picking some flowers to decorate the dining-room, it seemed she accidentally stumbled across the corpse, lying where it had been left by the murderer on the previous night at the foot of the drainpipe, with its hideously distorted features and sightless eyes turned up to the summer sky. Small wonder she rushed back into the house again in shock.

Now having been deprived of his night's rest, Charteris was not quite so gentle with Joan as he might have been. His irritability soon changed into something quite different, however, when he'd heard what she had to say. And accompanied by the indefatigable Kennedy, who had that moment arrived, he went to investigate the truth of her story.

One look at the remains of poor Ferguson was sufficient corroboration for anybody. It also spelt adieu to all hopes of sleep, so far as Inspector Charteris was concerned.

The news spread like wildfire. And within an incredibly short space of time, all the occupants — with the exception of Lady Gertrude, who was once again barricaded in her room — were aware of this, the latest tragedy to take place in their midst. The details were received by everybody with horror; particularly in little Tommy's case, since he overheard it being discussed on his way down to breakfast.

The whole establishment was by this time in a state of undisguised turmoil. And if the servant problem had been acute before, it was certainly doubly so now — which possibly accounted for the perfectly foul repast which the inspector, badly in need of nourishment to sustain his nearly exhausted nerves, was forced to partake of in lieu of breakfast.

It was halfway through this sombre meal that he remembered his promise to ring the Yard, and made his way hurriedly to the phone. On being put through, he was relieved to learn that Jackson had not yet shown up. In point of fact, although he did not know it at the time, his phone message anticipated the latter's arrival by barely five minutes.

This settled, the inspector next turned his attention to the formalities concerning the removal of the body to Canterbury. Then, when he was just about to yield to Kennedy's repeated suggestion that he should take a couple of hours' sleep, Doctor Meredith arrived, bringing with him the results of the autopsy. These were all that it required to complete the inspector's morning.

In brief, stripped of all medical technicalities, the report boiled down to two bald statements, both equally unpleasant to the officer of the law: one, Miss Harcourt had been killed by a dose of some mysterious poison, the exact nature of which they were not yet able to determine, but which produced similar effects to those of strychnine; and two, there was no trace of either this or any other foreign body in the dregs of coffee that had been submitted for analysis. How had the poison been administered, then? Charteris shook his head and confessed himself floored. True, it might have been hidden in her food, but all chances of substantiating that theory were past, as a careful examination of the domestic staff soon proved to them.

By the time all these things had been attended to, it was the lunch hour. And still no word from Jackson! In the midst of this sea of mystification, the inspector found himself looking towards that young man as his one ray of hope. If he failed him, then he was beaten indeed. Never before had he felt so completely out of his depth as at the present time. And Kennedy — what must he be thinking about it all? As his introduction to Yard methods, he could scarcely have picked upon a more disastrous case. And to the frayed nerves of the inspector, his very quietness seemed an accusation in itself!

Lunch proved just about as gloomy as it was possible for it to be. No attempt being made at conversation, they each sat wrapped in their own thoughts, which, if the melancholy expression of their faces could be taken as any criterion, were far removed from pleasant. Even the absence of Jackson would have passed unnoticed, had not Joan commented upon it with a mild display of curiosity. Her mind was soon set at rest by the inspector, who told her that her cousin was merely engaged upon a little private investigation elsewhere. They all seemed far too apathetic to be inquisitive. And Charteris, in no mood to be gratuitously informative, made no effort to enlighten them.

As soon as the meal was over, Hoffman began making preparations for his departure; preparations which, although he promised faithfully to return that night, the inspector could not help but regard with uneasiness. There being nothing he could do about it, however, he was forced to let it pass. For in absence of actual proof against anybody in particular, they were all at perfect liberty to come and go as they pleased.

No sooner had Hoffman departed than Joan and Pat announced their intention of taking Tommy out for a walk. Considering all the child had been through in the last few days, it seemed a very excellent plan, as did that of allowing him to appear in the village concert that evening along with Pat. This despite the fact that the committee organising the concert had been on the phone protesting against such a course to Joan most of the morning. Anything to take his mind off the unpleasant happenings which were going on around him seemed the order of the day, so the inspector raised no objections to the proposed expedition. At last, left to themselves, he and Kennedy retired to the study, where they awaited with obvious impatience the return of

Conway Jackson.

That young man, in defiance of a wracking pain somewhere in the region of his head, had taken the road in his immaculate Alvis during the early hours of the morning, according to schedule. The drive, as he'd anticipated, did him good. The storm having cleared away overnight, the countryside was fresh and verdant; while a light breeze had replaced the stifling heat of the last few days, carrying with it an invigorating tang from the moist earth. Speeding down the narrow lanes, it was not long before his mind began to function easily and logically again, thereby enabling him to apply all his energies to the case in hand.

Soon he found himself in the outer suburbs, the roads of which were already beginning to grow congested with the morning traffic. And having arrived thus far, it was not long before he was in the great metropolis itself, where, regardless of the earliness of the hour, the air was filled with the thunder of innumerable vehicles.

At Scotland Yard he was treated with all

civility. As has been mentioned before, this was not his first connection with the forces of justice; a fact they had not forgotten. His work there accomplished, he climbed back into the sports car, and once more took the road.

From London it might quite naturally have been supposed that he made his way straight back to Hamlin Hollow and from thence to Gleeson Manor, where his old friend and colleague Inspector Charteris awaited his arrival with such trepidation; but this was not the case. Instead of making for Hamlin Hollow, he directed the shining nose of the Alvis towards Canterbury. One stop at a garage, and another at a country pub, where he partook of a hasty and frugal meal, constituted the only breaks in his journey. It was early in the afternoon when he entered the cathedral city and drew up before the police station.

With a determined look upon his pale face, he entered the building and made his enquiries of the desk sergeant, which soon resulted in another interview with Rogers. At first, the ex-butler greeted him surlily, expressing, in none too polite terms the desire to be left to himself. But Jackson took no notice of this, proceeding more roughly than was his wont to the business in hand.

His opening question sounded as surprising as it was direct. 'What do you know about the woman who called herself Miss Harcourt?'

The man showed a glint of uneasiness, and then straightaway took refuge behind his mask of sulkiness. 'Nothing,' he replied, casting his eyes down at the floor.

'I wonder if it would assist your memory in any way if I was to tell you that somebody murdered her last night?'

'Murdered her? Good Lor'!'

'I thought that might surprise you. So now perhaps you'll try to help me find her murderer — since nothing you say can do her any harm? It might be a good idea if you started by telling me exactly why you let her steam open my telegram.'

'Was it yours, sir?'

'It was.'

Gone was all trace of belligerence, and now the man seemed thoroughly scared, and only too eager to get the information off his chest as quickly as possible. 'I didn't mean to do it, sir; honest I didn't,' he protested whiningly. 'I was trying to run straight — '

'Until you set eyes on Miss Gleeson's diamonds and Mr. Hoffman's pearl studs! I know all that. Inspector Charteris told me. But tell me about the time when you met Miss Harcourt before.'

'Why, I'd known Jeanne Treville — or Harcourt, as she called herself — for years,' the man declared, hastily correcting himself. 'But I thought she'd left the country.'

'She had. Go on!'

'So when I saw her posing as a governess, I wondered what she was up to. And I faced her with it. But she said she was trying to earn an honest living, same as me.'

Jackson smiled. 'Of course she did. And you believed her?'

'Yes. Poor sap that I was!'

'Well?' Jackson persisted.

'For a time everything seemed O.K. And then this business of the letter cropped up.'

'The one addressed to me?'

Rogers nodded. 'She made me hand it over, threatening that unless I did, she'd give me away to the master. Well, I'd no choice, had I? He'd most likely have taken her word against mine. So I let her have it. And when she'd finished, she gave it back to me.'

'Having steamed it open in the meantime?'

'Yes, sir. But I had nothing to do with that. Then she said I was to try to listen in to all the master's phone conversations; and that if any letter came for him, I was to let her have it first.'

'Which you did in the case of mine?'

Rogers lowered his eyes again.

'Yes, sir.'

'Was that all you did?'

'Yes, sir.'

'Sure?'

'Quite sure, sir.'

'Then the only letter you intercepted was the one to me?'

'That's right, sir. Sir James didn't often write letters — he said he hated 'em.'

'Hm! I think you've been truthful up

till now, but I want you to think very carefully before answering my next question.'

'What's that, sir?'

'Can you remember if Miss Harcourt — we'll call her that for the present, anyway — ever gave you the slightest hint as to her reason for wishing to have Sir James's movements so closely watched?'

'No, she didn't, sir.'

'Would you swear to that?'

'Yes, sir. I asked her lots of times, but she refused to tell me anything.'

Jackson looked a little disappointed. 'Just one more point,' he went on. 'Did you get the impression she was working for herself or for somebody else?'

'I didn't ever think about it, sir.'

'Cast your mind back a little way, and try to remember how long ago it was that you first met her.'

Rogers thought for a moment or two before replying. Then: 'About three years, sir.'

'Not less?'

'No, sir. Longer, if anything.'

'And in those days, did she work by herself?'

'I think so, sir.'

Jackson picked up his hat. 'Thanks, Rogers,' he said pleasantly. 'I think that's about all, always supposing you haven't been keeping anything back.'

'I haven't, sir, I swear.'

'All right then. By the way, I suppose your reason for remaining silent before was because you didn't like the idea of being a squealer?'

'That's right, sir.'

'No other reason, was there?'

'No, sir. On my word of honour.'

'That'll do, then.'

A few minutes later he left the police station, and this time turned the Alvis in the direction of Gleeson Manor. It was just after three o'clock when his car slid up the tree-lined drive to come to rest before the impressive portico. And on gaining admittance, he made his way to the study, where he joined the other two, who were still awaiting his return.

'Well, Jaggers?' Charteris boomed out almost as soon as he'd entered the room.

'Thanks for ringing up the Yard,' Jackson retorted easily, seating himself.

'My visit proved most helpful.'

'Your theory's worked out, has it?' the inspector enquired eagerly, and Jackson nodded. 'You know what you said before you went?'

'About giving you the murderer?'

'Yes. Do you know who it is?'

'I do. But please don't ask me to divulge it to you yet.'

The inspector threw up his hands in a gesture of exasperation. 'Good heavens, man!' he cried irascibly. 'We've been sitting here the whole afternoon like a couple of stuffed dummies, waiting for you to return. And when you do, all you say is that you've found the murderer but don't want to divulge his identity to us just yet!'

'I know how you feel, Charteris,' Jackson sympathised. 'But you see, although I know who it is, I've no actual proof against him yet. And so until I have, it seems that the fewer people know about it the better. One thing I can tell you, though, is that the woman we knew as Miss Harcourt was in reality a small-time crook by the name of Jeanne Treville. They had her record and photograph at the Yard. And Rogers admitted that he recognised her the moment she stepped foot in the house.'

'Rogers did?' The inspector pricked up his ears sharply. 'Have you been over to Canterbury as well, then?'

'I have,' Jackson retorted with a rueful smile, 'in spite of receiving a nasty crack on the back of the head last night, which nearly prevented me from going anywhere — except perhaps the gates of paradise, or the other place.'

'How did that happen?'

'Simplest thing in the world, I assure you. Just like this.' Briefly he recounted the incidents that had befallen him on the previous night. And as he did so, the inspector's eyes opened wide with astonishment. He had just concluded his recital when the sound of a door being banged brought Charteris to his feet.

'Just a minute, Jaggers,' he excused himself. 'That may be Meredith. He said he might look in again.'

Hastily he made for the door, the other two following close upon his heels. But when he threw it open, no grey-haired medico was revealed to them, but the slim figure of Joan Gleeson, hurrying across the hall. Something odd about her demeanour immediately roused Jackson's curiosity, and he ran after her.

'Joan!' he called.

At first she paid no attention, although she must have heard him, but started mounting the stairs.

'Joan! Joan!' he repeated from the centre of the hall; and she started, as though coming out of a trance.

'Is anything wrong?' he asked, addressing the question to her averted back.

'I — I don't know,' she replied in a harsh cracked voice, quite unlike her own. Then she turned; and he was horrified at the change in her.

'I — I think I'm going mad!' she whispered, fixing her wild eyes upon his. He opened his lips to say something — words of consolation, in all probability; but before he could make any suitable rejoinder, she had run swiftly up the stairs and vanished from his sight. The distant slamming of a door told him that she had shut herself in her room.

17

A Silk Stocking

Jackson turned back to Charteris with a perplexed shrug of the shoulders. This behaviour from Joan of all people, who had until now appeared so perfectly level-headed, seemed incomprehensible. He was about to say as much to the inspector when he was interrupted by a sharp knocking at the front door. Without waiting for the arrival of one of the servants, he strode across the hall and threw it open. Outside stood Pat Burke with Tommy.

'Have you seen Joan?' the young man enquired hastily as they stepped across the threshold.

'Yes. Just a few moments ago,' Jackson told him.

'Did you — did you notice anything odd about her?'

'Odd? How exactly do you mean?'

'Well, she — '

'Here, hold on a minute! Come into the study.' Jackson's reason for stopping him at this point was not far to seek; the sudden appearance of a parlour maid for the purpose of answering the door providing the explanation. 'Right you are. Tommy, you wait for me in your room, will you? I shan't be long.'

Obediently the child moved to the stairs, as Jackson dismissed the maid and turned with the others towards the study. Directly the door was closed behind them, the conversation was resumed.

'Go ahead!' Jackson directed.

Pat, a puzzled expression clouding his habitually frank Irish eyes, proceeded to do so. 'Well, the three of us went out for a walk this afternoon, as I expect you already know,' he began. 'You see, we thought it'd be a good thing for Tommy to get away from the house for a bit. Joan seemed perfectly all right at first — a little depressed, of course, but that's quite natural under the circumstances. But on the way back she became rather pensive, so I slipped my arm round her waist.

Tommy, noticing this, jumped up and kissed her, saying 'cheer up' or something of the sort; and I did likewise. Suddenly I felt her whole body stiffen. Then, without a word, she broke from my arms and ran away home. And — and that's about all there is to it,' he concluded lamely.

Jackson, to whom this narrative conveyed absolutely nothing, looked to Charteris to see what effect it had produced upon him. But to his surprise, the inspector did not appear nearly so flabbergasted as he'd expected him to be.

'I don't see it's so very peculiar, Mr. Burke,' he rumbled soothingly. 'After her experience of last night, I don't expect she relishes the idea of being kissed by anybody — with all due respect to you.'

'That seems a little unfortunate for Mr. Burke,' Jackson put in facetiously. 'But what precisely was her experience last night?'

When the inspector had told him the whole story, however — beginning at the time when he received a blow on the arm from the now-deceased gardener — it was Jackson's turn, for once, to look amazed;

and for the first part of the recital he certainly did. Although at the conclusion he seemed strangely perturbed, despite his glib assurance to Pat to the contrary.

'There you are, Mr. Burke; I think that about explains it all,' he said, assuming a lightness he was far from feeling. 'I shouldn't worry about it, if I were you. She'll recover. After all, you can't expect her to have a shock like that without experiencing some after-effects, you know.'

'I suppose not,' Pat retorted unhappily.

'Of course not,' the inspector added his assurance to Jackson's; the truth being that he had perceived an intent look in the latter's eye, and was anxious to get him alone. 'You run along, and think no more about it. And whatever you do, be sure not to refer to it the next time you see her.'

'Very well. Thank you, gentlemen.'

But for all his attempts to see things from their point of view, it was nevertheless a sadly unconvinced and harassed Pat Burke who slipped from the study to join Tommy upstairs as he'd previously arranged.

'This puts the whole thing in an entirely different light,' Jackson was saying. 'It makes it even more serious than I'd anticipated.'

'To which are you referring?' enquired the inspector. 'Miss Gleeson's unfortunate experience, or the murder of Ferguson?'

'Miss Gleeson's experience, of course,' Jackson retorted surprisingly. 'In the case of Ferguson, it's obvious what happened. He probably tried to polish off the murderer by himself, and the tables were reversed upon him. That's not what worries me. It's not likely to have any far-reaching consequences — but the other is; how far-reaching it's difficult to say.'

The telephone clamoured sharply, and Kennedy, being the nearest, picked up the receiver. 'Hullo . . . ? Yes . . . ' He looked towards Charteris. 'For you,' he said briefly.

Charteris took the receiver from him; and there followed a short conversation, after which he replaced it with a look and a gesture very akin to despair. 'From

Meredith,' he volunteered. 'They've made a second analysis of those coffee dregs. Nothing in them at all.'

Kennedy scratched his head in a way betokening the extreme mental irritation he was going through. 'Then, how on earth *was* she killed?' he demanded of the two mute occupants of the room as he sank into the nearest chair with a profound sigh.

His query was received in dead silence. Then: 'Great Scott! Why didn't I think of it before?' Jackson burst out impulsively.

'Think of what?' growled the inspector.

'Her stockings, of course!'

'Her stockings? Are you going mad?'

'No. Don't you see — ' He was cut short by a gentle rap at the door.

'Come in!' the inspector bawled out ungraciously.

The door opened a few inches to admit the slim figure of Pat Burke.

'What do you want?'

'I came round to let you know that Tommy and I are going down to the village for tea. I thought you might wonder what had become of us,' he explained quietly. 'Afterwards we shall probably drive around in the car until it's time for the show, things being as they are.'

'What show?' asked Jackson hastily.

'The village concert we're appearing in. It's tonight, you know.'

'Of course. I'm sorry; I'd forgotten.'

'That'll be all right, Mr. Burke,' the inspector told him civilly enough. 'Thanks for letting me know.'

'Not at all.'

No sooner had the door closed upon him than they reverted to their former discussions.

'What were you saying before we were interrupted?' Charteris enquired sharply.

But in the interim it seemed Jackson had recovered from his excitement and become more secretive. 'It doesn't matter now,' he replied evasively.

This time the inspector really looked upon the point of exploding. His face had turned a dull shade of purple, and his words tumbled over one another in a disordered rush for articulation. But Jackson, apparently quite unmoved by this perfectly warrantable exhibition of temper, cut him short.

'Will you do me one last favour?' he asked with an air of unusual gravity.

The inspector paused, awed by the other's tone, and his expression of irritability was quickly replaced by one of resignation. 'Very well, go ahead,' he answered weakly. 'You're my only hope, so I suppose I'd better humour you.'

''Humour me' is right! Will you two keep watch and see I'm not disturbed while I search upstairs?'

'What d'you want to search upstairs for?' the inspector demanded in a feeble attempt to have his curiosity appeased.

'The reason doesn't matter — yet. But if I find what I'm after, the mystery surrounding the death of Miss Harcourt will be a mystery no longer!'

'I see,' the inspector said, nodding his head. 'Something about her stockings, eh? Though what in heaven's name they could have to do with her being poisoned is beyond me! It's her room you want to search, I suppose?''

'Yes.'

'Well, you're not likely to be disturbed.'

'Is everything just as it was at the time of her death?'

'Exactly. Nothing's been moved.'

'Good. Now you two keep a keen lookout in case anybody tries to come up. Be sure nobody gets up those stairs until I've finished.'

'But why all the secrecy?' put in the inspector with a slight return of his former irascibility. 'Nobody's liable to barge in on you up there.'

'That doesn't mean they might not come across me in the passage; and I don't want to arouse any suspicion. That clear?'

'Yes. Go along and have your fun! Kennedy and I'll loaf about the hall and see nobody disturbs you.'

'Thanks.'

'Are you sure you'll be able to find the room?' the inspector enquired as they made their way across the hall a few minutes later. 'Or shall Kennedy come up and show you the way?'

'I can find it,' Jackson assured him confidently. 'Remember I had a good look at that map of yours, and I know the positions of all the bedrooms by heart now. Besides, we went up together last night.'

'Smart lad,' retorted the inspector with just a ghost of a twinkle in his steady eyes. 'That's what comes of using the grey matter.'

For a split second Jackson's features relaxed into a friendly grin, but it was so quickly over that it might never have taken place at all. As he turned and ran lightly up the stairs, his face was set in the same grim lines as before, and its expression did not change one iota throughout what followed.

What he had said about being confident concerning the positions of the bedrooms was not a piece of mere bravado, as was proved by the direct way in which he proceeded to his objective. Opening the door softly, he slipped into the dead woman's bedroom, closing it behind him. Illuminated as it was by the warm afternoon sunshine, it seemed hard to believe that only a few hours ago it had been the scene of death; a strange and unnatural one at that! Yet it had been the case. And the pleasant apartment, with its beige-coloured walls, light paint and attractive modern furniture, must contain somewhere a clue that would lead to the solution of the tragedy; of this Jackson felt convinced.

His bright eyes darted hither and thither, holding a glint of enquiry in their shadowy depths as they settled momentarily upon each and every object in the room. Then, starting with the drawers in the dressing-table, he began his search. Like that conducted by the inspector upon the previous night, it was meticulous to the nth degree. Only, there was one great difference between them: on the former occasion, Charteris had been looking for anything in the nature of a clue that he could find, but in the present instance Jackson was looking for something in particular that he knew the room must contain.

After several minutes he lighted upon it in the corner of the wardrobe among a little heap of dirty clothing. The things he drew out into the light caused a momentary gleam of triumph to flit across his face; the next second, however, he was by the window examining them as though they had been some priceless objets d'art, yet with all the trained impersonality of the investigator. Thoughtfully he drew one of the silk stockings over his hand until, near the heel, he came across a large rent big enough to put his four fingers through.

With furrowed brows he regarded the tear for some time in silence. And as he did so, a light began to dawn over his features. A curious excitement showed in his eyes too, as a sharp exclamation broke from him. Withdrawing his hand and rolling the stocking up into a neat ball, he thrust it into his pocket and turned towards the door.

It was about twenty minutes after his ascent that he appeared again at the head of the stairs, to the obvious relief of the two men waiting below, who were by this time heartily sick of their imposed watch. In silence they made their way back to the study, where Jackson, without waiting to be asked, plunged straightaway into a detailed analysis of a theory concerning the death of Miss Harcourt, which held his hearers spellbound.

At first the inspector felt inclined to dismiss the whole thing as a piece of fantastic rubbish, but as Jackson went on to unfold it piece by piece, in calm, incisive tones such as might have been employed with advantage by any barrister-at-law, their incredulity gradually vanished. And soon they were as convinced of its validity as the narrator himself.

'I'm sorry if you've found it boring mounting guard down here, gentlemen,' he apologised politely. 'But if it's any consolation, I can assure you that your patience has not been tried in vain. All I need now is the confirmation of the police surgeon — Meredith, I believe you said his name was? — to be able to prove to you, beyond all shadow of doubt, the devilish and ingenious method by which the woman we knew as Miss Harcourt met her death. In the present emergency, however, I don't propose to wait for that confirmation, but am going to lay before you what I believe to be the true facts, here and now. But before we start, here are two exhibits which I should like you to examine.'

From his pockets he took first the torn silk stockings he'd been looking at upstairs; and after this, something they soon identified as the slightly distended horseshoe sometimes found fixed upon the toes of heavy walking shoes. Beside this he set the three screws that had been used for holding it in position. Whilst the two men were staring at these objects, he took up his stance by the fireplace.

'The first thing I want you to note is the hole in that stocking,' he went on after a break of a few seconds. 'You will remember,' he addressed himself to Charteris, 'we were told yesterday afternoon that Miss Harcourt had laddered her stocking. A gross underestimate, as you can see for yourself. You will doubtless agree that far from being a ladder, it's a large tear, which must have been caused by something sharp. And surely something sharp enough to cause a tear of those dimensions must have also scratched the flesh underneath a little? That's not wrenching at the bounds of possibility in any way; it's more improbable to suppose it could be otherwise.'

'I'm just beginning to see what you're driving at,' the inspector growled as his interest grew more intense.

'I wonder if you are? Now, according to Doctor Meredith's analysis, Miss Harcourt was poisoned. But so far as we can judge, the fatal dose does not seem to have been administered either in her food or in her drink. What is the other alternative then? There is only one; it must have entered her system through a scratch.'

A grunt from Kennedy broke in on his discourse, whilst Charteris nodded understandingly.

'It goes without saying that the murderer didn't wish to arouse the suspicions of his intended victim. So what did he do? Simple. He arranged the whole thing to look like an accident. We're fairly safe at this point in taking it for granted that Miss Harcourt was his accomplice; and as such, she was not to be disposed of so easily as the others.

'What follows may sound far-fetched at the moment, but I'm convinced the doctor's analysis will bear me out. Having a quantity of deadly poison in his possession — how and for what reason I don't pretend to explain, it being of no especial significance at this point — the murderer proceeds with the following design. First, he loosens the centre screw of that toe cap you see before you. Loosens it, mark you — not removes it. He loosens it until it stands out about a quarter of an inch from the sole — the position it was in when I removed it from the shoe a few moments ago, with the invaluable assistance of a screwdriver that lay conveniently to my hand. Then, putting on the shoes, he strolls downstairs.

'And here comes the second part of the story. Waiting for his opportunity, he bends down, unobserved by the lady, and anoints the screw with a thick solution that he's already prepared for the purpose. By a carefully staged stumble or something of the sort, he manages to catch the screw top in the heel of her stocking — you'll notice that it's been deliberately made jagged at the edges. He apologises for his clumsiness; and either then or later — it's impossible to tell which at the moment — she retires to change her stockings, carrying in her veins the deadly dose! All quite simple, gentlemen; and, if we're lucky, capable of substantiation by Meredith.'

'What a fiendish idea!' murmured Kennedy in a hoarse whisper.

'It's plausible,' assented Charteris. 'Weird but plausible.'

'The only danger lay in the delayed action of the poison; this being possibly due to the smallness of the amount capable of being administered on a screw top,' said Jackson thoughtfully.

'I'm inclined to believe you're right, Jaggers,' the inspector decided.

'I know I am,' the other told him calmly. 'Remember, truth is often much stranger than fiction. And I'm willing to swear that the man from whose shoe I removed those screws is the murderer we've been looking for — the terror of Gleeson Manor! The Vampire Man!'

18

Fatal Blunder!

The sincerity of these last words set at rest any lingering doubts they might still have been nursing, and from that point onwards they were prepared to eat out of his hand. Which was just as well; for the scheme he was about to unfold was destined to test even their faith in him almost to the breaking point.

During the silence that ensued, Jackson slipped quietly from the room, leaving the two officials to chew over what he had told them. With sureness of purpose, he made his way to the stairs, which he ran up nimbly two at a time until he reached the first landing. And here again his extraordinary photographic memory came in useful. For he went, without the slightest trace of hesitation, to a door on the left.

Raising his hand, he knocked lightly on

the wooden panel. After a few seconds, he received a reply.

'Who's there?' enquired a feminine voice from within.

'It's Jaggers.'

'You can't come in!' The words sounded sharp, like a rasp of despair.

'All right, Joan,' he answered soothingly. 'I don't want to come in. I only want to know if you'd like a lift down to the village tonight. Pat and Tommy have gone already, but — '

'I don't want a lift, thank you.'

'But, my dear, you don't propose to walk to the concert, do you?'

'I'm — I'm not going to the concert.'

'Not going?'

'No!'

'Are you quite determined about that? I mean, it'd be a pity if you changed your mind after I'd gone.'

'I shan't change my mind. I tell you I'm not going!'

'Very well; just as you please.'

'Do you mind going away?'

'Of course not — if you feel like that about it. Sorry I troubled you!'

In contrast to the annoyance conveyed by his words, Jackson's face as he turned from the door and made his way back to the study showed signs of relief, as though things were going just as he wished them to. Back in the study, he found the two inspectors still enthusiastically discussing his theory; a discussion that stopped at his entrance.

'We both feel you're dead right, Jaggers,' Charteris informed him while he took up his former position by the fireplace. 'So the sooner we get that stocking to Meredith for analysis, the better.'

'Just one minute.' Jackson's voice, although low, held a distinct note of authority in it; and the two men looked to him with single accord. 'You'll never know how grateful I am for the generous way in which you've taken up my theory,' he went on hastily. 'It makes it so much easier for me to say what I have to say. When I persuaded you both to mount guard for me just now, I said it was the last favour I should be asking of you. I'm afraid that was too optimistic an estimate, for I am about to ask you another favour at this very moment. And it's the greatest one you've ever had to concede to me.'

Inspector Charteris did not waver for an instant. His eyes, which had sought and found Jackson's, remained fixed upon them unblinkingly. 'Well?' he queried.

'I want you both to put yourselves entirely in my hands,' the other continued a little breathlessly. 'To do what I ask you unquestioningly and in the blind belief that what I'm doing is right. I know it's presumptuous of me to ask this, but — '

'Cut the cackle, Jaggers,' snapped the inspector. 'We agree to the first part; tell us the second.'

'Very well; I'll start with you then. I want you to have dinner with me tonight at the Kentish Arms. We can look in at the doctor's on the way, if you like. You look after the stocking, and I'll take care of the other exhibits. They'd be no use to Meredith, because you can see they've been recently cleaned. I would have returned them, but unless I'm very much mistaken, we shall have captured the murderer before he has time to discover his loss.'

'That sounds hopeful, anyway. And

what do we do after dinner?'

'We're going to the village concert in Hamlin Hollow.'

'The what?' the inspector began incredulously.

But Jackson held up a finger in admonition. 'Don't forget your pledge,' he reminded him. 'You were to put yourselves entirely in my hands.'

'I know; but village concerts at a time like this!'

'I warned you that it might be difficult.'

'So you did. All right, then. Go on!'

'That's all so far as you're concerned — for the moment. Now for you, Inspector Kennedy.'

Kennedy was already leaning forward in his chair, hanging eagerly upon his hero's every word. But if he'd hoped for excitement, he was doomed to disappointment.

'You are to stay here, Inspector Kennedy. After dinner, I want you to return to this room. You will switch all the lights out, leaving the door open, and seating yourself in a position from whence you can command an uninterrupted view of the hall. Is that clear?'

'Quite, Mr. Jackson.'

'Thanks for listening so patiently, both of you.' He turned to Charteris. 'And now, I think we may as well get started.'

The inspector rose obediently to his feet. 'Seems about all we can do,' he remarked drily as he and Jackson transferred the exhibits to their pockets.

'Afraid you're in for a rather lonely dinner, Inspector,' Jackson remarked sympathetically to Kennedy as all three together they made their way towards the front door. 'Lady Gertrude and Joan will most probably dine in their rooms, if they dine at all; and everybody else'll be away.'

'That's all right, sir,' retorted the inspector cheerfully. 'I only hope something happens!'

'If that's what you want, I don't think you're going to be disappointed,' the other returned grimly.

A few seconds later, Jackson and Charteris were seated in the former's luxurious car, speeding in the direction of the village. Throughout that drive neither of them spoke, for each was too preoccupied with his own thoughts; the inspector wondering what Jackson was up to, and Jackson himself offering up a silent prayer that his little ruse might succeed.

Their first stop was at Doctor Meredith's. His establishment happened to be on the outskirts of the village, and they were lucky in finding the grey-haired practitioner at home. To the stocking, which they duly produced for his inspection, he showed not the slightest reaction at all. In fact, Jackson was privately of the opinion that had they presented him with a couple of bloodstained bones, he would have shown no greater interest. He seemed to be just that sort of person. After he had promised to let them have the results of the analysis at the first possible moment, they took their departure.

The first thing to strike them both simultaneously on arrival at the Kentish Arms was an air of unusual bustle and activity. The doors giving on to the street having been thrown open on account of the heat, a jumble of noisy chatter and laughter reached their ears. Driving down the little alley at the side of the building, they found the gate standing open, and

Jackson turned the car into the yard beyond. Shutting off the motor, he and the inspector alighted.

The fact that he made no attempt to garage the car in the red brick shelter provided for the purpose struck Charteris as being curious, although with an exemplary display of tact, he avoided remarking upon it. In answer to their summons, the side door was opened by Judy, looking extremely pretty and a little flushed, as though something exciting were happening. When she learned that Jackson wanted a meal for two served in his room as quickly as possible, some of this gaiety vanished. But on being assured that anything would do so long as it was edible, she brightened up considerably and promised to do her best.

In the meanwhile, for the purpose of killing time until the food arrived, the two men betook themselves to the bar. And here the reason for Judy's excitement became all too plain. No sooner had they stepped foot over the threshold than they were surrounded by a mob of bright and inquisitive young men. Everybody seemed to be talking at once, and few words were audible above the tumult beyond one or two meagre scraps such as ' . . . exclusive story . . . give us the lowdown . . . greatest scoop in years . . . ' from which it could be gathered that the gentlemen of the press had descended upon them, en masse!

In the case of Sir James, Charteris had been rather clever in getting rid of them; but now, with four murders on his hands, nothing short of a miracle could have saved him from their attentions, and well he knew it. They were obliged to spend a very hectic twenty minutes before finally retiring to Jackson's little room, where a simple but appetising dinner awaited them. But during that time they managed to accomplish something; between them they succeeded in persuading the reporters to keep away from the manor by the simple expedient of telling them that everybody had been allowed to leave. Although this was not strictly true, it nevertheless served its purpose, and the majority of the reporters seemed quite content to confine their search for copy to the village, at any rate for the present.

The greatest coup of the moment appeared to have been the location of the maid who had walked from Gleeson Manor to Hamlin Hollow on the previous evening. This young woman happened to be a friend of Judy's; and already picturing herself as a much-publicised heroine in the columns of their daily press, she was bursting to tell her story. From the point of view of Jackson and the inspector, she was a gift from the skies; and, although completely unaware of it, she was assisting in keeping the press away from them in the most effective way possible.

Dinner over — and a very delectable feast it had been too! — they found they'd just sufficient time for a cigarette before sallying forth to the hall next door.

'What time do you generally bolt that gate leading into the back yard, Judy?' Jackson asked the barmaid casually when she came to clear away the coffee cups.

'Closing time, sir,' she answered promptly. The 'sirs' had crept back for the inspector's benefit.

'That's ten o'clock down here, isn't it?'

'Yes, sir.'

'Do you think you could leave it open a little longer tonight? I may want to get my car out in a hurry.'

'Oh yes, sir. I'll leave it open until you give me the word, if you like.'

'Good.' Soon after she had left them, they rose to go.

'Isn't there anything you want to tell me, Jaggers?' the inspector enquired hopefully as they moved towards the door.

Jackson turned and regarded him thoughtfully. 'No, not right now, Charteris,' he replied slowly. 'Tonight's happenings will show you who your murderer is without my telling you.'

And with that the inspector had to be content. Not wishing to attract the attention of the reporters again, they avoided the bar and slipped out the side way. Already several cars were lined up along the narrow alleyway, and amongst them they both recognised Pat Burke's old four-seater.

Skirting the main entrance to the Kentish Arms, they found themselves in front of the hall: a long, low wooden structure outside of which several unevenly lettered bills — the paint having run rather badly in the recent rain — announced 'A Grand Charity Concert'. Making his way to a little table in the curtained-off section that served as an improvised vestibule, Jackson succeeded, after a short parley with a very fat lady arrayed in the most striking example of a renovated pre-war gown he could ever remember setting eyes upon, in acquiring — for the sum of one-and-sixpence each — a couple of seats in the third row from the front. Wondering why his companion wanted to be so near, yet refraining from worrying since he was not called upon to pay for his seat, the inspector followed Jackson moodily down the centre gangway.

They had no sooner seated themselves than the entertainment began. The opening, as is often the case in affairs of this kind, was performed by the local vicar. And if anything could have been more conducive to sound undisturbed slumber than his wearisome address, the inspector had not heard of it.

The vicar having been disposed of, the

turns followed one another with monotonous regularity, each a little duller than the one preceding. From time to time, Charteris stole covert glances at his companion; but beyond a mild and tolerant expression of amusement, the latter's features told him nothing. Restlessly he turned from side to side in his uncomfortable wooden chair, and wished with all his heart for the finish. Had the auditorium been darkened, he would doubtless have succumbed to the desire aroused in him by the vicar at the beginning and indulged in a surreptitious nap; but since all the lights were left on, with the result that one was as clearly visible to those on the platform as to one's next-door neighbour, even this small solace was denied him.

The cream of the entertainment had apparently been reserved for the last turn but one; this being represented by Pat Burke and Tommy. And they certainly came up to expectations; Pat with his pleasantly Irish sense of humour, and Tommy with some really astonishingly fine vocalisations. It was the quality of the latter that resulted in several of the audience declaring afterwards that 'the boy must be a professional!' So good were they, in fact, that even those who had until this moment considered it a disgraceful thing for them to be appearing at all under the circumstances were enchanted; while the inspector, for the first time, found himself fully awake.

But as fate would have it, it was during this part of the programme — the only part which he could have wholeheartedly enjoyed — that Jackson elected to misbehave himself. With dramatic emphasis, he began whispering in the inspector's ear, at the same time indicating the pair on the platform. It was with a feeling of amazement that Charteris realised the lips moving so urgently next his ear were uttering no intelligible sounds. Then it dawned upon him — the whole thing was a fake! For some reason or other, Jackson wanted the people on the platform to imagine they were being talked about. Had it been anybody else but Jackson, he would have thought he was qualifying for an asylum. But remembering his pledge to help in every way possible, he did his best to provide suitable reactions.

How suitable they were was soon proved by Pat and Tommy, whose eyes kept wandering in their direction in a sort of comic perplexity. Owing to the absence of words in their discourse, it was completely silent; so apart from the discomfort they caused to the performers, the whole thing passed by their neighbours unnoticed: a clever piece of stage management on Jackson's part which the inspector, although completely in the dark, was not slow to appreciate.

The final turn, after Pat and Tommy had made their exit amidst the most prolonged burst of applause of the evening, was a ballad singer. And throughout her three songs and the subsequent dismissal by the vicar, Jackson behaved himself impeccably. It was only at the very end that he rose to his feet and suggested a visit to the dressing-rooms for the purpose of picking up their friends — if friends they could still be called, considering the unseemly behaviour they'd had meted out to them.

Obedient to the last, the inspector

followed at his heels, only to be informed that Pat and Tommy had already departed; a piece of news which, far from dashing Jackson's spirits, seemed to increase his strange excitement a thousandfold.

Once outside again, the inspector really felt that the time for a little questioning had arrived at last. And with this end in view, he framed his first query. 'Where do we go to now?' he ventured timidly by way of an opening.

'After them, of course,' came the brusque reply. 'Back to the manor!'

'But how can you be sure that's where they've gone to?' the other persisted feebly.

Instead of answering, Jackson let out a sharp exclamation of surprise. They had just entered the little alley beside the inn and drawn up behind the spot where Pat Burke's car had so recently rested stood the Alvis.

'Why on earth did they take it out of the yard?' the owner muttered savagely as they bore down upon it.

But the sounds of revelry that came to them from that same yard told their own story of how it had been converted into a temporary beer garden for the use of the reporters. 'And after all,' as Judy told him some hours later by way of explanation, 'you *did* say you might want to get your car out in a hurry, Mr. Jackson.'

In silence the two men climbed in, and with a muffled roar the Alvis sprang forward. Out of the village they swept, and along the deserted country road.

And then, without any warning, something began to happen — something so palpable that even the inspector, untutored in such things, could not fail to notice it. Their speed began to diminish in the most alarming way. And within a few minutes they had come to an abrupt standstill. With a cry of annoyance, Jackson jumped out and threw back the bonnet. It took only a very brief examination to tell him the worst.

'Water in the petrol tank. The car's been tampered with,' he announced tersely.

Almost as soon as he'd said it, the inspector was by his side. 'Do you suppose that was done to keep us away from the manor?' he asked.

'Of course it was!' the other replied miserably.

'Then you must have been on the right track all along!'

'From the very beginning! But I made one fatal blunder, and it'll probably ruin the whole thing. I should have locked up the car. My God! Why didn't I?'

'No use blaming yourself at a time like this,' the inspector retorted, suddenly catching the other's excitement. 'We've got to do something! How far is it to the manor?'

'About three miles, all uphill,' Jackson replied hopelessly.

'That's not far.'

'Take us the best part of an hour on foot. Long enough for something dreadful to happen. You don't understand — if we can't get there at once, it may be too late!'

As Charteris looked into the other's horror-filled eyes and realised the full purport of his words, he felt momentarily stunned. A tight grip upon his arm pulled him together.

'You were right just now when you said we must do something,' Jackson hissed close by his ear. 'We've got to get there. Pray to God we're in time!'

And with a look of fresh determination on their pale, set faces, the two men hurled themselves forward up the steep incline.

19

The Vampire Man

For Inspector Kennedy, his very worst presentiments seemed to be coming true. Jackson's gloomy prophecy concerning a solitary dinner was carried out to the letter; and for a naturally sociable being like the inspector, dinner alone in the vast dining-room at Gleeson Manor was no joke. If anything, the food was even less palatable than at lunch-time; or perhaps, being by himself, he noticed it more. At any rate, the recent events appeared to have thoroughly upset the cook, and the unwholesome food provided yet another excellent reason for everybody wishing to have the whole business cleared up at the earliest possible date.

After dinner, in accordance with Jackson's instructions he betook himself to the study, where he sat moodily sipping his coffee and smoking until nine o'clock;

when it was the appointed hour for switching off the light. This he did, opening the door and manoeuvring himself into a convenient position from which he could command an unobstructed view of the darkened hallway.

As the grandfather clock ticked away the minutes, his hopes of high adventure began to dwindle. Not daring to smoke, he sat on stiffly for an hour. At the expiration of this period, as testified by the silvery notes of the clock, he rose and took a few turns about the room, obediently returning a few minutes later to his seat. In one way the darkness was an asset, for it kept him on the alert, straining eyes and ears for the slightest indication of anybody approaching; whereas had he been called upon to perform the same task in broad daylight, he might easily have allowed his thoughts to wander.

As the clock in the hall proclaimed the half hour, its dying notes were swallowed up by a fresh sound. His instincts immediately on the alert, he craned forward eagerly to catch more; but at that moment it ceased altogether. That it had been the soft purr of a car, he was ready to swear. And moreover, it had come to a standstill outside the front door.

Getting to his feet, he gently pushed the chair away and flattened himself against the wall. The hall was so dark that he was unable to see the front door, but two slight clicks with an interval between told him that it had opened and closed. In a silence that was so intense he could almost feel it, Kennedy waited.

Presently, as though it were one with the shadows surrounding it, a dark curiously bent figure glided across the hall and up the stairs. The darkness and the distance combined to render it indistinguishable, but no sooner had it disappeared than the inspector tiptoed from his hiding-place in pursuit. Stealthily he mounted the stairs, being careful to pause every time one of the treads creaked — a not infrequent occurrence, considering the staircase happened to be an extremely ancient one — and eventually he reached the top.

Taking his foot off the last step, he stood looking about him, wondering which direction his quarry could have chosen.

The next second the problem was solved for him in a manner that was as decisive as it was unpleasant. Without the slightest warning, something heavy crashed down upon his head. There was a feeling as though his skull were caving in, followed by a blinding flash of light — and with a low moan, Kennedy sank unconscious to the floor!

★   ★   ★

To Joan, in the seclusion of her room, the hours dragged by in an agony of uncertainty. Dinner, she flatly refused. And she either sat on her divan, or wandered restlessly up and down; seeking, amid the welter of sensations which threatened to overwhelm her completely, some way out.

How true, she reflected bitterly, are some of those trite old sayings we all too eagerly dismiss as being platitudinous. The saying to which her mind kept constantly reverting in the present instance was 'ignorance is bliss'. Possibly, it was a bit of an exaggeration; but 'bliss' or not, her former existence had been vastly preferable to what she was going through at the moment. For now she knew the truth — or part of it; and the knowledge appalled her!

By pure accident, she had stumbled across the identity of the thing she secretly thought of as 'the soft horror', the revolting creature that had crawled on to her bed during the dark watches of last night. And the mere knowledge somehow served to make her feel morally unclean.

Had it been a stranger she could have handed over to the authorities without thinking twice about it, the situation would have been different. But as it was, something stronger than herself was holding her back. What should she do? A little voice somewhere deep down inside of her counselled slyly: 'Why do anything at all?' But to this sort of advice she turned a deaf ear, knowing that if she followed such a course and the atrocities continued, she would be condoning them. And such a thought was abhorrent to her.

At last, when the twilight had deepened into darkness, she arrived at a decision. So far she had only learned half the truth;

but it was within her power to discover the rest. That it might make things even more distasteful than they were at present, she was fully aware. But since almost anything seemed better than this soul-wracking inactivity, she took her courage in both hands, and carefully unlocking the door, let herself out into the dark passage.

Knowing that if she hesitated she was lost, she ran as hastily as her legs would carry her across the polished boards in the direction of her stepmother's bedroom. Here she paused, a gentle rap on the door eliciting an immediate response.

'Who's there?' demanded a startled voice.

'It's Joan. I must see you!'

In answer to her demand, the sound of a key grating in the lock was borne to the ears of the trembling woman in the darkness outside; and the next moment the door was cautiously opened. Impatiently pushing by, Joan made her way into the lighted room beyond.

'Well?' demanded her ladyship at once, closing the door and following her stepdaughter into the circle of light cast by the lamp on the small table beside the old oak bed.

Joan turned and faced her, a glint very like defiance flashing from her beautiful eyes. 'I know!' she announced dramatically.

'Know? What do you know?' enquired Lady Gertrude in a voice which, despite all her efforts to keep it even, held a distinct tremor.

'I know who murdered my father!' Joan flung back at her passionately. 'I know who murdered them all! I found out this afternoon. And I've come to ask what sort of hold he has over you to make you keep silent all this time. You've got to tell me! I must know, or I feel I shall go mad! I simply must know!'

'Don't worry, my sweet! You'll know soon enough,' a strange masculine voice purred at her from behind. Simultaneously, the two women swung round in the direction of the door, Lady Gertrude remembering on the instant that she'd forgotten to relock it after Joan's entrance. But now it was too late!

Leaning nonchalantly upon the handle, a curious short figure clothed in a long dark overcoat that reached to the floor, and wearing a black felt hat pulled well down over his brows, stood surveying them with cynical amusement. It was not possible to distinguish his features owing to the shadows, but it was comparatively easy to make out the dull gleam of an automatic; and upon this both women found their attention immediately riveted.

The glint of defiance had died out of Joan's eyes on the instant, its place taken by an expression of horrified revulsion. As for Lady Gertrude, she remained rigid as though tensed to endure whatever might be coming.

The figure advanced a few paces into the room, but not far enough to dissociate itself entirely from the protecting shadows. 'Not like you to leave your door unlocked, my dear Lady Gertrude,' it sneered in a horrid rasping voice. 'I suppose it was Joan's fault. Really, my dear, you shouldn't upset your stepmother so; she can't stand it!'

'How did you get here?' The voice

which asked this was Joan's, but it was so distorted as to be almost unrecognisable.

'Why, the same way as I left, of course,' the figure retorted with exasperating slowness. 'By car.'

'But — '

'I know what you're worrying about, my dear. And I'm going to be kind and put you out of your misery. I haven't killed him. I should have done, only I realised it would only make you dislike me more than you do already. So I refrained, and merely laid him out with the aid of a rather heavy spanner instead. He'll be all right when he comes to; the only disadvantage from his point of view, of course, being that he won't come to for quite a long time.'

'You monster!' There was more than a hint of tears in her voice; and her tormentor, noticing this, seemed to regard it as a sign of victory, for he emitted a low chuckle.

'Please let's avoid melodramatics!'

'What have you come back for — that's what I want to know,' said Lady Gertrude with ominous calmness.

The black figure shifted its piercing gaze from Joan and fixed itself upon her. 'And a very sensible question too,' he declared. 'For the very simple reason that, having some regard for manners, I did not like the idea of leaving this charming retreat without first bidding adieu to my hostess.'

'So Jackson's frightened you, after all!' she taunted him with a cracked laugh.

'"Frightened" is too powerful a word. Let's say I've decided that discretion is the better part of valour.'

'When do you leave?'

'At once. There's no time to lose.' The reply was like a shot from a gun; and Lady Gertrude smiled.

'Most discreet of you, I'm sure. So nothing remains now but that we wish you bon voyage — after you've extracted the usual promise of secrecy from us, of course?'

The figure slowly shook its head; an ordinary enough action, but one that seemed to carry some dreadful implication with it. 'Your promise will not be necessary, Lady Gertrude.'

Joan raised eyes that had suddenly become filled with speechless terror. 'You wouldn't — ?'

'Of course he would,' her stepmother cut her short, catching hold of a chair back to steady herself. 'He'd kill me without giving it a second thought.' The lips that framed the next question had turned an ugly shade of purple. 'And what, may I ask, do you intend to do about Joan?'

There was a moment's silence while the eyes switched over to the shrinking woman in the corner. Then: 'She conies with me!' the voice replied in a tone that had grown insidiously caressing. 'You see, strange though it may seem, I happen to be in love with her.'

'Are you mad?' gasped Joan as she instinctively cowered still further out of the light.

'Because I say I'm in love with you? Come now, that's being too modest!' The voice dropped to an even lower key, and its suave silkiness took on a more intimate note. 'Why do you think I kissed you last night when I thought you were asleep?

Because I needed you so badly that I couldn't stay away. I came to you — '

'With the blood of a poor defenceless old man still fresh on your hands!'

'Poor and old he might have been, but not so defenceless, believe me! He attacked me first, and he was really quite strong.'

'You ought to know I'd rather die than go with you!'

'That, I think, is an exaggeration.' The automatic moved gently in the darkness, as though its owner were toying with it. 'Anyway, I don't propose to give you the choice.'

A low moan broke from Lady Gertrude as she sank limply into the nearest of the upright chairs. During the last few minutes, the mauve tinge of her lips had deepened, and her face had begun to quiver spasmodically. Suddenly her head fell awkwardly to one side. With a cry of alarm, Joan ran to her assistance.

'Stay where you are!' hissed their captor dangerously. But she paid no attention to him.

The next moment a strong hand

pushed her roughly out of the way. 'I said stay where you are!' the voice grated in her ear whilst the cold nose of an automatic wormed itself firmly into the small of her back. 'Put your hands behind you!'

Wretchedly she complied, and soon felt them firmly tied together with a length of something that bit into her wrists. All at once, a thought flashed through her brain — so horrible that it was all she could do not to cry out. As she turned her head, the black figure behind her read what was in her thoughts before she had time to give it utterance.

'You're wondering if I'm going to do away with her before she recovers consciousness, aren't you?' the voice sneered. 'You'll see, my angel.'

A numb, cold horror started to steal over her limbs as she felt herself being pulled backwards towards one of the darkest corners in the room.

'Sit down,' the voice commanded.

And when she resisted, she was thrown brutally into a chair.

'I can see I shall have to teach you a

little obedience,' he snarled. 'Open your mouth!'

Searching fingers holding something soft were already feeling round her lips.

'Open your mouth!'

With all her strength, she buried her teeth in the fleshy part of one of his hands.

With a muttered curse, he dropped the gag to the floor. For a second or two, he nursed his injury in silence. Then, walking round to the front of her: 'You've asked for it, and you're going to get it!' he snapped; and the next moment a blow that brought tears stinging to her eyes landed on her cheek. 'That's lesson number one!' Without repeating his order to open her mouth again, the gag was retrieved from the floor and rammed between her teeth. 'Better tie your feet up too, and carry you to the car,' the voice continued viciously.

Through a haze of pain, she saw him produce some cord from one of his pockets, and soon her slim ankles were lashed tightly together.

Backing away from her, the strange

figure, whose face was still in the shadows, surveyed his handiwork. 'Splendid,' he murmured appreciatively. 'And now, if you're sensible, you'll close your eyes for a few minutes. What I'm going to do won't be exactly what you'd term pleasant; not at all suitable for a sensitive young lady like you. You can't scream,' he reminded her, 'and this automatic of mine is fitted with a silencer. So take my advice, and don't look.'

Her own pain swallowed up in a greater terror for her stepmother, Joan felt herself alive and tingling in every nerve. Desperately she tried to cry for help; but not a sound beyond a muffled croak could she give utterance to.

Slowly and deliberately the figure had turned from her and was now advancing, with fiendish fixity of purpose, upon the prostrate woman in the chair. With every ounce of strength left in her body, Joan wrenched at the cords that secured her wrists. But with each movement they grew tighter, and soon a stream of warm blood was oozing unheeded down to her fingertips.

Through the open window, a cool gust of wind came and blew her hair gently to and fro against her damp forehead. Wildly her eyes travelled round the room — and then they remained rooted; fixed upon the door with a sort of hypnotic fascination. For it was moving! Unbelievable though it seemed, it was opening, inch by inch, slowly but surely!

The form of her captor was within a few paces of Lady Gertrude, the automatic gleaming evilly in his hand, when he became aware of the opening door also. With a sharp intake of breath, he wheeled round just in time to see a burly figure slip into the room. With a cry of rage, he fired. The figure dropped, and the bullet buried itself in the wall behind him. He had raised his hand to fire a second time when an answering shot rang out from the direction of the window. With a shriek of pain he let his automatic clatter to the floor, as Conway Jackson, with one swift movement, sprang clear of the sill!

What followed, Joan could never clearly remember. All she knew was that instead of two rescuers, there were suddenly three; the third, a vaguely familiar figure, having appeared in the doorway behind the first.

After a brief struggle, they succeeded in getting their prisoner safely handcuffed. And while Jackson speedily and with many expressions of concern undid her bonds, the other two men, whom she now recognised as Inspector Charteris and Fritz Hoffman, dragged the sinister black-coated shape into the light. As Charteris jerked off the man's hat and tilted the lamp full in his face, both he and Hoffman gave a horrified gasp of surprise.

'Now you know why I wanted some proof before I told you who he was,' Jackson called out over his shoulder as he helped Joan to rise.

'But — but, Jaggers,' the inspector floundered in bewilderment, 'how on earth did you manage to find him out?'

And well he might have asked such a question! For the figure that stood between them charged with so many crimes was none other than the person they had known as Tommy, the child of ten. Now a child no longer, but a man; or rather, a raging, frustrated animal whose hideously snarling mouth and hate-filled eyes were revealed for the first time in all their stark ugliness by the white beam from the lamp.

A slight groan prevented Jackson from answering, and turned everybody's attention to Lady Gertrude. 'She's coming round,' he murmured as he moved swiftly to her side. He turned to Joan; but before he could get out what he was about to say, a dreadful laugh cut through the stillness with the sharpness of a razor blade.

'She'll have to stand her trial as well as me!' shrieked the figure between the two men. 'She's in it as much as I am! She'll pay for it, blast her! She'll pay for it!'

And with the most malicious and devilish laughter shaking his whole frame, the small figure, which might well have been the personification of all evil, was hurried from the room as Lady Gertrude gave way completely in a sudden rush of tears.

20

'Till the Next Time!'

It was some hours later that Jackson returned to Gleeson Manor in his long-bodied Alvis, which was by this time running as smoothly as ever. He did so in answer to a pitiful entreaty from Joan, which came to him over the phone in the little police station in Hamlin Hollow; where, so he informed her, they had 'Tommy' Drew, a man with a criminal record, aged thirty-eight, under lock and key.

According to Joan, as a result of the stress of the last few hours, the manor was still in a state of chaos; and she implored him to come over and explain away some of the doubts that were keeping them all from their beds, despite the lateness of the hour.

Putting aside the attraction of a comfortable bed awaiting him at the

Kentish Arms, Jackson promised to do so. And thus it happened that, with the first tinge of dawn barely lighting the eastern sky, he was once more driving along the uneven road to Gleeson Manor.

Inspector Kennedy, whom they found lying insensible out on the landing, had already been removed to hospital in Canterbury. The blow he'd received had been a severe one, and for some time to come his condition was likely to remain serious. Pat, whose condition did not give so much cause for alarm, was being treated at the manor. Inspector Charteris on the other hand, had retired to bed as soon as he'd seen to it that Thomas Drew, having duly made and signed a statement setting forth all his misdeeds, was safely incarcerated in the one cell the station boasted.

The Alvis had no sooner come to rest outside the stately portals of the manor than the door was thrown open, and Joan came running down the steps to meet him. Amid a shower of thanks, he was led into the lounge, where Pat, his head bound in a most workmanlike bandage

— the result of Joan's unaided efforts, and Fritz Hoffman awaited him with steaming coffee and biscuits.

Upstairs, Lady Gertrude, attended by Doctor Meredith and a nurse from Canterbury, lay between life and death. That last shock had proved too much for her, and the doctor had already confided in her stepdaughter that he held little hope of her recovery, although he was doing all within his power to save her.

As soon as he had warmed himself with his coffee and was drawing contentedly at a cigar given to him by Hoffman, Jackson took pity on his audience and prepared himself to answer the unspoken deluge of queries he could so clearly see were forthcoming.

'How did you come to suspect Tommy in the first place?' Joan started the ball rolling by unconsciously repeating Charteris's question of only a few hours ago. She couldn't bring herself to call him anything but 'Tommy', for the name came naturally to her.

'By several isolated incidents, which at the time seemed to lead nowhere,'

Jackson explained slowly. 'The first thing to strike me was that not one of the people who broke into the study immediately after Uncle James's murder could possibly have been the culprit. Nobody could have killed him and joined the others without attracting attention. And Tommy was the only person who never put in an appearance.

'The next thing was that fiendish laughter, brought about no doubt by a curious brand of cynical delight inspired by my departure, which Charteris and I heard on my first night down here. It seemed to come from the house; and Tommy's bedroom, as I subsequently learned, was at the front. He, Miss Harcourt and Lady Gertrude, with the exception of the servants, were the only people not to be accounted for either in the music-room or the back garden, at the time.

'These were small enough points in themselves, but added to the fact that the murderer was described to me on two separate occasions as 'a bent figure . . . running close to the ground', they began to make sense. Both Ferguson and Uncle Frederick had noted this fact. Now, why should the figure stoop? To disguise its identity? That's possible, of course. Certainly nobody in the house — and we soon ruled out the possibility of the crime having been the work of an outsider — suffered from a stoop.

'But if it was being used by the murderer to mask his real identity, why should he bother about it on occasions when he had every reason to believe he was unobserved? Precaution, you'll say at once; but to a person not used to stooping, it's an extremely tiring attitude to assume, and definitely not one to be adopted except when vitally necessary.

'All this, added to the fact that in the case of Uncle Frederick the body showed signs of having been sprung upon, led me to the supposition that the person we were after was not a man with a stoop at all, but a dwarf! And, moreover, a dwarf with fairly long fingernails — as testified by the torn lapels of Uncle Frederick's coat, which I noticed at once that day I paid my first visit to Canterbury.'

At this juncture, Joan gave a sharp exclamation of surprise. 'Had I known that earlier,' she cried, 'I might have discovered his identity last night!'

'Oh? Why?' enquired Pat.

'Because before I went to bed,' she told him, 'I noticed a long scratch on the back of my hand, and I couldn't remember where I'd got it. Now I know it must have happened when I was trying to calm him down after his nightmare.'

'And a very clever ruse for disarming suspicion that was,' said Jackson, taking up the narrative again. 'With all due respect to him, I must say that for a grown man, he carried it off extremely well. I suppose he thought it was just what a child might do under the circumstances, so he set about it without delay.

'But I discovered something on that night, the same as Joan might have done had she possessed sufficient knowledge of the case. It happened when I lifted him off the stairs. I noticed he seemed rather heavy. It was this which first made me seriously suspect him; and on going over the details I've just given you, I found that several of them confirmed the idea. Despite his carefully staged nightmare, he saw by the expression of my face that I'd discovered something, and as a result decided to pay me a little impromptu visit at the Kentish Arms later in the evening. It was a lucky thing for me that I happened to be awake to receive him!'

'But how does Miss Harcourt come into this?' asked Hoffman, speaking for the first time.

'She comes into it both as his accomplice and his wife.'

To say that this announcement caused a sensation would be to underestimate its effect; but Jackson went on with apparent unconcern.

'The first lead to her came from Uncle Frederick's story of how he'd seen the black shape swarming up the drainpipe to her bedroom. The next was the fact that until recently she'd had dyed hair — a most unusual procedure for a governess. And finally, her dummy spectacles turned up, showing beyond all shadow of doubt that for some reason or other she'd been disguising herself.

'Having arrived so far, I felt justified in removing the photo from her room — the one she'd disliked you taking so much, Joan. And no wonder! At the Yard, I had no difficulty in identifying her as a crook who usually went by the soubriquet of Jeanne Treville — a discovery that clinched all my suspicions concerning her, and shed a sinister light upon her association with Tommy. Unfortunately I came across no mention of him. I did not know at that time, however, that they'd only come into contact in Paris a few months ago.'

'But what motive was there behind all these crimes?' asked Pat.

'Motives,' Jackson corrected him. 'In this case, as in several others, one murder automatically led to another. We'll start at the beginning with Sir James. The motive behind his death was a very common-place one: he knew too much! Unluckily for him, he overheard an incriminating conversation between Tommy and Lady Gertrude. Even more unluckily, from his point of view, Tommy saw him walking away; and by the look on the baronet's face, he immediately guessed what had happened.

'For safety, he set Miss Harcourt to shadow him; and she, in her turn, put a little pressure on Rogers. Thus it happened that Sir James's letter to me was intercepted before it left the house. And my answer unwittingly set the time limit to a crime that had already been planned. All this has been proudly confessed by the horrible creature himself in his statement down at the station. Terrified of remaining in his own bedroom, Sir James crept downstairs and locked himself in his study, where he was ruthlessly done to death! So ended the first chapter.

'The second chapter concerned Uncle Frederick. From Lady Gertrude, Tommy learned that Frederick Gleeson had seen him entering Miss Harcourt's bedroom, and already suspected his identity. When Tommy saw him from his bedroom window setting out for the Kentish Arms, therefore, he quite rightly jumped to the conclusion that he was going to hand on some of these suspicions to me. He judged the man correctly in suspecting that he would not divulge the whole thing at once, but resolved nevertheless to kill him on his way home, before he had a second chance to do so. It was on this occasion that he was forced to strangle Ferguson's dog also.

'And that brings us to the murder of his wife. The motive behind this was quite different from the others.' He fixed his eyes upon Joan. 'Although they'd only been married for a few months, he wanted to get rid of his wife in order to be free to make off with you, my dear. After your experience of last night, you can't be ignorant of what his feelings were. I regret to say they were responsible for his planning and perpetrating the most fiendish crime of all!

'Being naturally observant, in common with others of her class, his wife soon sensed his preoccupation with another woman. And this resulted in violent scenes between them, as upon the afternoon when Charteris and I waylaid her in the study. On that occasion, she said she was going upstairs to get a book;

whereas, in reality, she was escaping for a few minutes from an extremely unpleasant quarrel with her husband.

'That was before I'd begun to suspect him; and I must confess that when I spoke to him in the garden a few minutes later, he was as cool as though nothing in the world had happened. He even went so far as to tell us Miss Harcourt intended leaving, just to make things a little difficult for her.

'In view of this situation, however, his wife was well on her guard. There was no chance to kill her like the others, for her door was locked against him each night. So he had to think of something original; and he did!' Here he recounted in detail the series of events that had culminated in Jeanne Treville's untimely end.

'He used a poison he had come by when abroad, the fatal venom of the black mamba snake, which produces effects similar to those of strychnine. He made it into a paste, and managed to scratch her heel under the table in the music-room. It was performed so neatly that she never suspected him at all, but thought she'd torn her stocking on a screw sticking out from one of the table legs. And so she died, without giving him away. And that seems to be all, excepting the murder of poor old Ferguson, which is self-explanatory.

'Although it sounds straightforward enough now, I can assure you it was far from being so a few hours ago, when all the actual proof I had was that gadget taken from Tommy's shoe. It was in an effort to substantiate my theory that I very reluctantly decided to use Joan here as bait. The fact that she'd recognised in Tommy's kiss that afternoon the same nauseating qualities as in the illicit embrace she'd been subjected to during the small hours was a piece of luck, from my point of view. For it decided her to stay at home, and suited my purpose admirably.

'Taking Inspector Charteris with me, I went to the village concert; where, I regret to say, I misbehaved myself disgracefully. But ill-mannered though I undoubtedly was, there was method in my madness; the object of it being to convey to Tommy that I was on his track. This brought the result I'd anticipated.

'I purposely gave him a little while to get away; and, as I thought, he persuaded Pat to bring him straight back here; intending to make a getaway and take Joan with him. The one possibility I'd not taken into consideration was that my car might be moved out into the alley, thereby giving the murderer his chance to pour water into the petrol tank; which he did.'

'He must have done that while I was having a quick one at the Kentish Arms,' Pat exclaimed feebly from beneath his bandages.

'That's obviously what he did do,' Jackson agreed with a kindly smile. 'But you weren't to blame. It might have proved tragic though, had not Mr. Hoffman turned up on his way back from London and given us a lift; especially since Inspector Kennedy, who I'd left on guard, was so swiftly put out of action.'

'What gave you the idea of climbing in at the window, Cousin Jaggers, and how did you do it?' enquired Joan.

Jackson smiled. 'I just made up my mind that our enemy shouldn't have a monopoly on window climbing,' he replied lightly. 'As to how I managed it, that was quite easy. The inspector, Mr. Hoffman and I came in by the servants' entrance, so as to avoid making any noise. I went straight to Pat's room next door, and climbed from his window-sill onto Lady Gertrude's. It was pure luck that her window happened to be open; otherwise I should have had to break the pane, which would have warned him, and also given him time to get in a few more shots. Anything else?'

Joan shook her head contemplatively. 'No, I don't think so. That seems to make it all clear, except that I can't see his reason for coming here in the first place. And what I still want to know — ' she began, but Jackson interrupted her.

'You still want to know where your stepmother comes into all this,' he said quietly. 'And so do I! That's the one thing he's kept dark. But here, I think, comes our answer.'

His words referred to the figure of

Doctor Meredith, seen through the open doorway, descending the stairs. Coming to the threshold, he beckoned to Jackson and Joan, and they obediently followed him out into the hall.

'Lady Gertrude has been asking to see Miss Gleeson,' he explained to Jackson in an undertone. 'And she said that if you happened to be here, she'd like you to come up too. I've done my best to dissuade her, but she insists. She says she's something very important to tell you both. I can only ask you to be as brief as possible.'

Nodding their assent, they followed the lean figure of the doctor up the broad staircase and along the passage, stopping before the now familiar doorway leading to Lady Gertrude's boudoir. In silence they entered.

After a short consultation between the doctor and the very efficient-looking nurse, they approached the bed and stood waiting for her to speak. The doctor leaned over, whispering something in her ear, after which she slowly turned her eyes in their direction. On recognising her two visitors, she gave a slight smile; and, as though aware that she had very little time left at her disposal, she began to speak at once.

As she proceeded, her voice grew gradually weaker. But what she told them shed new light on the last dark recesses of the mystery of Gleeson Manor. 'I want both of you to listen very carefully to what I have to say,' she murmured, as with one white hand she beckoned them closer. 'Although the doctor here has tried to contradict me, I know that I'm dying! I've suffered with my heart for a great many years now, and the strain of these last few weeks has been too much for me. Before I go, however, I wish to clear things up.' Her next remarks were addressed to Jackson. 'I don't expect — Tommy . . . ' She paused before the name as though loath to utter it. ' . . . has told you why I've been shielding him?'

Jackson shook his head.

'I didn't think he would. He's saving it all for the trial. But as I won't be there, I want to give you my explanation — if any explanation is possible — now. It's all quite simple, really. You see, this hideously abnormal creature is my son by my first husband, John Drew.'

Both her hearers gasped, but she continued without paying any attention to them.

'I had not set eyes on him for a great number of years. He left me when he was still in his teens, shortly after his father's death, at the end of the war. I cannot pretend I was sorry to lose him; he had always been a torment to me, although God knows I'd done my best to be kind to him. I never mentioned him to Sir James or to his relations, because they were apt to look down on me as it was; and Tommy was never a son to be proud of, having disgraced himself by turning pickpocket even before he became sixteen.

'It was with a feeling of real panic, therefore, that I found myself face to face with him in Paris six weeks ago. He lost no time in torturing me afresh. It started with a little blackmail — he did not take long to find out that I was remarried and had kept his existence a secret! While I was there, he became involved in an unsavoury scandal. It was in connection with the night club where he appeared as a child impersonator (that was the only thing in which he was talented; he was able to perform even without the aid of make-up); and he and his wife, the woman we knew as Miss Harcourt, decided that they must flee the country. The first place they fixed upon was England — but there was a snag to it! Miss Harcourt — I'll call her by that name — could not return to England, for she had been deported only two years previously. It was then Tommy hit on the idea that he and his wife should come to Gleeson Manor, masquerading as my adopted son and his governess.

'At first I refused. But when he threatened to reveal his identity to Sir James, I consented on the condition that the deception last only for a few weeks, until they could find a better hiding-place. So it was all arranged, and — '

'Excuse my interrupting, Lady Gertrude,' Jackson put in softly, 'but what was Sir James to be told when your adopted son and his governess disappeared? They surely didn't intend to fade out without some sort of explanation?'

Lady Gertrude shook her head, and it was obvious that her strength, which had held out so splendidly, was beginning to wane. 'The explanation was arranged in advance,' she answered, quickening her pace. 'A note was to be left behind, purporting to have come from Miss Harcourt; in it she was to explain that she was really Tommy's mother, and that the whole thing had been an imposition started for the sole purpose of escaping from the French police. The last part at least was to be true!

'And so the deception began. They met me at Dover. How they succeeded in escaping from France, I don't know. And for a while everything went smoothly, until my husband began to suspect. There's no need to go into all the details leading up to his — his murder, because I expect you already know them.

'Although I was aware that he spent whole nights locked in his study, and should have sensed what was coming, his death stunned me just the same. But I soon realised how dreadful it would be if

I were to come forward and tell what I knew; not only for myself, but for Joan also. And so I started my ill-fated policy of suppressing information and forcing others to do the same.

'Then came the second murder; and I saw that whereas before I'd had a certain amount of choice in the matter of telling what I knew or keeping silent, I now had to keep quiet whether I wanted to or not, for the moment I came forward I should be running the risk of being cited as an accessory. And that — that was my position until tonight; and a pretty pitiful tale it makes in the telling.'

Sinking back on to the pillows, she closed her eyes in an effort to check the sudden rush of tears that obscured them like a translucent curtain. Leaning forward, Joan kissed her impulsively on the cheek.

'Don't worry, darling,' she said a little tremulously. 'We understand.'

The dying woman opened her eyes and smiled faintly. 'Thank you,' she murmured. 'I swear I never knew he had that — that awful passion for you, my dear.

You do believe me, don't you?'

'Of course I do.'

'That must have been his reason for refusing to leave here, even after the arrival of the police.'

Her eyes sought Jackson's; and with a grave smile he took her hand and raised it to his lips. 'I think I know what you're thinking now, Lady Gertrude; but don't worry about it any more. After all, your behaviour to me can be easily construed as a compliment, you know. And being a very conceited person, that's exactly what I'm going to do.'

A few seconds later, he and Joan were again outside the door. As they descended the wide staircase, there was a thoughtful silence between them that neither seemed inclined to break, since they both felt they had been in the presence of death.

And their instincts had not played them false, as was shown soon afterwards. For as the sun rose that summer's morning, Lady Gertrude's sorely laden soul left her body and travelled into the regions beyond all human care and pain.

Thomas Drew duly stood his trial at

the Old Bailey; and so great was the accumulation of evidence against him that the result was a foregone conclusion. After a short tussle with the French authorities who wanted him on various charges, the death sentence was finally passed upon him. He paid the supreme penalty for his numerous crimes with the same uncanny fearlessness that had characterised him throughout his life; and neither at his trial nor in the prison did he arouse one gram of pity in anybody.

It was only a few days after the world had been rid of this inhuman monster that Conway Jackson and Inspector Charteris found themselves standing upon the platform at Victoria Station, both arrayed in silk hat and morning-coat, for the purpose of seeing a charming young couple off on their honeymoon.

Jackson had given Joan away; and a lovelier bride he had never seen. Unfortunately, Fritz Hoffman was unable to be present, as he'd already started on his world tour; but he sent the happy pair a handsome present nevertheless. Kennedy was there, though; only, being rather bashful, he slipped away before the reception.

Having come through all the unpleasant mud-slinging part of the trial with flying colours, Joan's beauty seemed in some strange way to have been enhanced instead of dimmed by the ordeal; and Jackson experienced an unusual pang of envy as he looked at the handsome, well set-up young man beside her.

As the train steamed out of the station, and the two men, feeling rather forlorn — as mere males are apt to do upon such occasions! — turned to go, Charteris put the standard question that he'd never failed to ask at the conclusion of any case in which he'd been associated with Jaggers. 'Not thinking of joining the force, I suppose?' he enquired tentatively.

Stepping into the shining Alvis which stood beside the kerb in the station yard, Jackson laughingly shook his head. 'Afraid not,' he replied cheerfully. 'Too much like work for me!'

'Where are you off to now, then?'

'To Scotland; to finish my interrupted holiday, of course. Cheerio, Charteris, till the next time!'

'Till the next time!'

With a wave of the hand, Jackson slipped in the gears, and the immaculate car rolled away.

'Queer cuss,' mumbled the inspector affectionately as he turned out of the station into the clear, bright sunlight.

The Alvis was now lost to sight, once in the stream of London's ceaseless traffic — and with it, as leisurely as he'd come, went Mr. Conway Jackson.

THE FACELESS ONES
GRIM DEATH
MURDER IN MANUSCRIPT
THE GLASS ARROW
THE THIRD KEY
THE ROYAL FLUSH MURDERS
THE SQUEALER
MR. WHIPPLE EXPLAINS
THE SEVEN CLUES
THE CHAINED MAN
THE HOUSE OF THE GOAT
THE FOOTBALL POOL MURDERS
THE HAND OF FEAR
SORCERER'S HOUSE
THE HANGMAN
THE CON MAN
MISTER BIG
THE JOCKEY
THE SILVER HORSESHOE
THE TUDOR GARDEN MYSTERY
THE SHOW MUST GO ON
SINISTER HOUSE
THE WITCHES' MOON
ALIAS THE GHOST
THE LADY OF DOOM

THE BLACK HUNCHBACK
PHANTOM HOLLOW
WHITE WIG
THE GHOST SQUAD
THE NEXT TO DIE
THE WHISPERING WOMAN
THE TWELVE APOSTLES
THE GRIM JOKER
THE HUNTSMAN
THE NIGHTMARE MURDERS
THE TIPSTER

With Chris Verner:
THE BIG FELLOW
THE SNARK WAS A BOOJUM

We do hope that you have enjoyed reading this large print book.

Did you know that all of our titles are available for purchase?

We publish a wide range of high quality large print books including:
Romances, Mysteries, Classics
General Fiction
Non Fiction and Westerns

Special interest titles available in large print are:
The Little Oxford Dictionary
Music Book, Song Book
Hymn Book, Service Book

Also available from us courtesy of Oxford University Press:
Young Readers' Dictionary
(large print edition)
Young Readers' Thesaurus
(large print edition)

For further information or a free brochure, please contact us at:
Ulverscroft Large Print Books Ltd.,
The Green, Bradgate Road, Anstey,
Leicester, LE7 7FU, England.
Tel: (00 44) **0116 236 4325**
Fax: (00 44) **0116 234 0205**

Other titles in the
Linford Mystery Library:

THE MISTRESS OF EVIL

V. J. Banis

John Hamilton travels to the Carpathian Mountains in Romania, along with his wife Victoria and her sister Carolyn, to research the risk of earthquakes in the area. The government provides lodgings for them in the ancient Castle Drakul. Upon investigating a disused basement room, the trio discover a skeleton in a coffin with a wooden stake through its rib cage — and Carolyn feels a strange compulsion to goad John into removing it. Soon afterward, a sinister visitor arrives at the castle — claiming to be a descendant of the original Count Drakul . . .

THE GREEN MANDARIN MYSTERY

Denis Hughes

When a number of eminent scientists — all experts in their field, and of inestimable value to the British Government — mysteriously vanish, the police are at their wits' end. The only clue in each instance is a note left by the scientist saying they have joined 'the Green Mandarin'. Desperate to locate his daughter, Fleurette, a Home Office official enlists the services of scientific detective Ray Ellis. But as his investigations get closer to the truth, will Ray be the next person to go missing?